Will Melanie leave Whitebrook?

"No racing," Melanie told Kevin when she led Trib outside. "Trib might buck me off."

"Would I do something like that?" Kevin asked.

"Yes." Melanie put on her helmet. Gathering the reins, she tried to imitate Kevin's mount. Only when she jumped up, she plopped across Trib's back and hung there like a sack. She grasped his mane with her left hand, pushed on his rump with her right, then swung her right leg over. When she finally sat up, her cheeks were flushed. Kevin had his head down, trying to hide his laughter.

"There's a phone call for you, Melanie," Ashleigh said as she strode over. She took hold of Trib's rein. "It's your dad. You can take it in the barn office."

"Dad?" Melanie was puzzled, then delighted. They'd had such a good time this weekend, she bet he was calling because he missed her.

Swinging her leg over Trib's rump, she dropped to the ground and ran into the office. The phone receiver was lying on the desk.

"Hey, Dad! What's up?" Melanie said when she picked it up.

"Hi, honey, I have terrific news," her dad replied.

"What?"

"Susan and I are getting married this weekend. We're going to be a family again. Melanie, it's time for you to come home to New York!"

THOROUGHBRED

A HOME FOR MELANIE

CREATED BY
JOANNA CAMPBELL

WRITTEN BY
ALICE LEONHARDT

HarperEntertainment
An Imprint of HarperCollinsPublishers

HarperEntertainment
An Imprint of HarperCollins*Publishers*
10 East 53rd Street, New York, NY 10022-5299

Produced by 17th Street Productions,
a division of Daniel Weiss Associates, Inc.

HarperCollins books are available at special quantity discounts for bulk
purchases for sales promotions, premiums, or fund-raising.
For information, please write:
Special Markets Department, HarperCollins Publishers,
10 East 53rd Street, New York, NY 10022-5299.

ISBN 0-06-106541-2

First printing: November 1998

Printed in the United States of America

Visit HarperEntertainment on the World Wide Web at
http://www.harpercollins.com

❖ 10 9 8 7 6 5 4 3

A HOME
FOR MELANIE

"GO, FAITH, GO," TWELVE-YEAR-OLD MELANIE GRAHAM cheered as she watched the three-year-old filly race around the training track. Leap of Faith stretched out, her pounding hooves digging into the soft dirt. Leaning low over Pirate Treasure's black mane, Melanie pretended she was the jockey and they were the ones galloping around the oval track.

Sensing her excitement, Pirate danced in place. "Easy, buddy." Melanie relaxed back in the saddle. "You know your racing days are over."

Pirate was blind. Before contracting the disease that had caused his blindness, Pirate had been one of the fastest horses at Whitebrook Farm, a Thoroughbred breeding and training facility in Lexington, Kentucky, that was owned by Ashleigh Griffen and Mike Reese, Melanie's aunt and uncle.

When the farm's vet had first diagnosed Pirate's problem, the handsome Thoroughbred had been turned out to pasture. He'd become depressed and listless, perking up only when Melanie walked him over to the track to be with the other horses.

Ian McLean, the head trainer at Whitebrook, had allowed Melanie and Pirate to pony racehorses. Now in the mornings, the two of them accompanied the young Thoroughbreds to and from the track and starting gate. It wasn't the same as racing, but Pirate enjoyed being back on the track and had regained some of his appetite and energy.

When Faith flew across the finish line, Melanie shouted, "Yes!" then steered Pirate over to the gap in the railing. Since Pirate couldn't see, he had to trust Melanie completely. Sometimes he would get nervous, especially if there were unfamiliar smells or sounds. But when Melanie used him to pony a horse, he always seemed to know that it was time to settle down.

"Great workout!" Melanie called to Naomi Traeger, Faith's sixteen-year-old exercise rider.

Grinning, Naomi pulled down her dirt-splattered goggles and let them drop around her neck. "She ran like the wind!"

Still excited by her gallop, the chestnut filly jogged through the gap in the fence. Naomi steered Faith next to Pirate, who stood quietly even when the filly bumped into his side. Reaching down, Melanie snapped the lead line onto Faith's bit.

"She's full of herself," Melanie said.

"That's for sure." Naomi let her reins go slack. "I'm glad I have you and Pirate to get me back to the barn."

"Are you through for the morning?"

Naomi nodded. Yesterday it had rained, and she was covered with mud from head to toe. Unsnapping her helmet, she let the strap dangle. Naomi was small, with a muscular build. A long dark braid hung down her back. She was a natural athlete, and Melanie loved watching her ride.

When they reached the training barn Melanie held on to Faith while Naomi dismounted. Whitebrook had three barns arranged in a horseshoe, and this morning the grassy area in the middle bustled with activity. Mares and foals were being led into the main barn to spend the hot day out of the sun, and the two- and three-year-olds in training were being cooled down and hosed off before getting their breakfasts.

When Naomi led Faith away, Melanie dismounted, too. She'd ponied four horses that morning, and though it wasn't as tiring as a riding lesson, she'd been in the saddle since six in the morning. Now it was almost nine, and the summer sun was getting hot.

"I bet you're ready for a brushing and some hay, too," Melanie said to Pirate. The big horse rubbed his forehead against her shoulder. The flies had been bad, and his eyes were tearing.

"We'd better clean out your eyes and put some medicine in them," she added. Pulling the reins over his head, she led him into the training barn. The barn was dark, and fans whirled overhead, so it was as cool as a cave.

After untacking Pirate, she put on his halter and hooked him to crossties in the middle of the aisle. Only then did she pull off her helmet. Her cropped blond hair was plastered to her head with sweat. She ran her fingers through the short mop, knowing there wasn't much she could do to make it look better.

Since he'd only walked and trotted, Pirate wasn't too hot, and a good rubbing with a towel followed by a brushing removed the marks left by his saddle. Melanie picked out his feet, then got his medicine from the supply room.

Pirate was like a big puppy dog—until she tried to put the ointment in his eyes. Then he would raise his head as high as he could, making sure there was no way she could reach him.

"This time I'm not giving up," she warned as she carried over an empty bucket.

She set it in front of him, turned it over, and climbed on top. "Now hold still, silly." She tried to squirt some ointment in his eyes, but he shook his head as if to say, *No way.*

Ten minutes later she'd succeeded in getting a little of the sticky medicine in one eye—and a lot all over her fingers. With a sigh, Melanie dropped her arms. As soon as Pirate realized she'd given up, he lowered his head, nuzzling her in the stomach as if to apologize.

4

"You didn't win yet." Reaching around to the back pocket of her jeans, she pulled out a chunk of carrot and held it under his nose. When he smelled it, his ears pricked forward. He lipped it from her hand, and while he was crunching, she quickly squeezed ointment in the other eye.

"There!" Melanie smiled triumphantly. The thud of hooves on the aisle floor made her look over her shoulder.

"You're going to spoil that horse," Naomi said. She was walking Faith around the barn to cool her off.

"He already is spoiled," Melanie replied as she jumped off the bucket. Pirate must have heard or smelled Faith, because he gave a low nicker of greeting. Raising her head, the filly nickered back.

"How was her time?" Melanie asked.

"Great. Tomorrow we're going to have a practice race with two of the other three-year-olds. I hope you and Pirate can pony us. Every time you two have accompanied us to the gate, we've done great. You're our lucky charm."

"Sounds good to me." Melanie grinned as Naomi led Faith in the other direction. Lately she *had* been feeling lucky. Not only was she enjoying Pirate, but she'd had a great visit this weekend with her dad and his girlfriend, Susan. Then she and her cousin, Christina Reese, had gone to a super party.

It's about time things went my way, Melanie thought. Since spring, her life had been full of ups and downs.

The ups had been great. But she wanted to forget the downs.

"Melanie! Are you going to Mona's with me?" a voice hollered from the far end of the training barn. It was Christina.

"No!" Melanie shouted back. "I'll see you afterward."

Several times a week Christina rode her Thoroughbred mare, Sterling Dream, to Gardener Farm for lessons with Mona Gardener. Christina was really excited about combined training, a sport also known as eventing.

In combined training, the horse and rider competed in three "tests"—dressage, cross-country jumping, and show jumping. Earlier in the summer Christina and Melanie had attended a riding camp to improve their eventing skills.

Christina had come back from camp and entered a local event at a nearby farm. In contrast, Melanie never wanted to ride another sitting trot or half halt. Ponying racehorses on Pirate had been the perfect break for her.

"Then how about a trail ride with me?" Kevin McLean, Ian McLean's twelve-year-old son, asked. Startled, Melanie turned to see where he was. She spotted him halfway down the aisle, leaning over the bottom half of a stall door. His baseball cap was turned backward and his auburn hair poked from beneath it.

"Have you been in that stall the whole time?" Melanie asked.

6

He nodded. "Yeah. You and Pirate have some interesting conversations. Though I did notice you do all the talking."

"Oh, shut up." Picking up a plastic currycomb, Melanie wound up and pitched. It flew through the open top door. Kevin ducked at the last minute, and it missed him by an inch.

Snorting nervously, Pirate pulled back on the crossties. "Whoa." Melanie laid her hand on his neck. "I'm sorry. I forget how skittish you can be."

He rolled his eyes, pawed the floor, then gradually relaxed. Melanie mentally kicked herself. She knew not to roughhouse around the horses, especially the Thoroughbreds. They were too big, high-strung, and unpredictable.

Unsnapping Pirate from the crossties, she led him by his halter to his stall. A flake of hay was waiting in the back corner. Melanie let go of the halter, watching as Pirate ambled inside. Swinging his head from side to side, he used his sense of smell to search for the hay. When he found it, he grabbed a big hunk and chewed greedily.

"So how about a ride before it gets too hot?" Kevin said in Melanie's ear. She whirled in surprise.

"Don't sneak up on me like that!" Melanie gave him an annoyed look. But she wasn't really mad.

"I sneaked up on you because I didn't want to be clobbered with a currycomb again," Kevin said, giving her a lopsided grin.

Melanie smiled back. "Sure, I'd love a trail ride. Trib needs some exercise. He's getting a huge belly."

"Okay, meet you in the main barn in fifteen minutes."

Melanie watched him leave, then put away her tack and grooming bucket. As she strode across the grassy area to the barn housing the mares and foals, she spotted her aunt and uncle talking to George Ballard, the manager of the stallion barn. Her aunt was frowning. Running a farm like Whitebrook was a lot of work, and one thing Melanie had learned about Ashleigh and Mike was that they were fanatics about the care and training of their horses. It had paid off, too. Whitebrook was known all over the country for its fine Thoroughbreds.

When Ashleigh saw Melanie, her frown changed to a smile, and she waved. Melanie waved back, and her uncle gave her a thumbs-up sign. "Good job this morning!" he called.

"Thanks!" Melanie called back with a grin. The other thing she'd learned about Ashleigh and Mike was that they were a great aunt and uncle. Since she'd arrived, they'd treated her with respect and kindness.

And even though she and Christina had gotten off to a rough start, they'd become close, too. In fact, Melanie realized, it hadn't taken long for her to think of Whitebrook as her home.

Kevin was already leading his horse, Jasper, from the barn. "Did you brush him?" Melanie asked as she patted the Anglo-Arab's neck.

"Naw. He's clean."

"You're going to ride in cutoffs?"

"I'm tough. Besides, I'm going bareback." Kevin walked around to Jasper's left side. Springing up, he whipped his right leg over Jasper's rear and landed softly on his back.

Melanie hurried into the tack room to get Trib's bridle. When she opened his stall door, the black-and-white pinto gave her a sour look.

"What? No happy whinny of greeting?" Melanie pretended to be shocked, though by now she knew what to expect. Tribulation—Trib for short—had been Christina's pony until she outgrew him. Since Melanie was smaller than her cousin, the two were a perfect match in size as well as personality. Trib was as ornery as Melanie.

"No time for brushing, but I do have this." She took a chunk of carrot from her back pocket. Instantly his ears pricked forward.

"I knew you loved me," Melanie teased, and giggled as he took the carrot. She put the reins over his head and, when he was through chewing, put the bit in his mouth.

"No racing ahead," Melanie told Kevin when she led Trib outside. "Trib might buck me off."

"Would I do something like that?" Kevin asked.

"Yes." Melanie put on her helmet. Gathering the reins, she tried to imitate Kevin's mount. Only when she jumped up, she plopped across Trib's back and

9

hung there like a sack. She grasped his mane with her left hand, pushed on his rump with her right, then swung her right leg over. When she finally sat up, her cheeks were flushed.

Kevin had his head down, trying to hide his laughter.

"Make sure you buckle those helmets," Ashleigh said as she strode over. She took hold of Trib's reins. "There's a phone call for you, Melanie. It's your dad. You can take it in the barn office."

"Dad?" Melanie was puzzled, then delighted. They'd had such a good time this weekend, and she bet he was calling because he missed her.

Swinging her leg over Trib's rump, she dropped to the ground and ran into the office. The phone receiver was lying on the desk.

"Hey, Dad! What's up?" Melanie said when she picked it up.

"Hi, honey. Hey, I have terrific news," her dad replied.

"What?"

"Susan and I are getting married this weekend. We're going to be a family again. Melanie, it's time for you to come home to New York!"

2

SPEECHLESS, MELANIE PLOPPED INTO THE DESK CHAIR. Home to New York? Her dad married? What was he talking about?

"Mel? Did you hear me?" she heard her father ask. "I said Susan and I are getting married. We're going to have the ceremony over Labor Day weekend—probably on Sunday. That'll give you time to get settled at the apartment before you have to go to school on Tuesday."

"You didn't mention getting married when you were here," Melanie pointed out.

"I know, sweetie. We didn't decide until the plane ride home. Neither of us can wait for you to get back here."

"But I *like* living at Whitebrook."

"I know you do. But summer's over now, and you need to get back to school. Besides, I miss you. I want you here with me—with us."

Melanie felt trapped. What could she say? That she didn't want to go back to New York? That she'd rather stay with her aunt and uncle and go to school with Christina?

Yes, say it. But the truth was that she missed her dad, too. And she knew it would hurt him if she said she didn't want to live with him.

"I know this is all sort of sudden," he continued. "Let it sink in a little, and let's talk again tonight. I need to talk to Ashleigh and Mike, too. We want them to come for the wedding. I want Mike to be my best man."

He rattled on excitedly for a few more minutes, but by then a fog of disbelief had spread over Melanie and she had tuned him out.

"So tell your aunt and uncle everything, and I'll call you tonight," her dad finished.

"Uh, right, Dad," she said, adding hastily, "And congratulations. You sound really happy."

"I am, Mel. Susan's great. I think you'll grow to love her as much as I do."

Melanie said good-bye, then slowly hung up. She couldn't believe it. This morning she'd been floating on a cloud, thinking how perfect her life was. Now, with one telephone call, she'd plummeted to the ground like a popped balloon.

For a few minutes she sat in the chair, numb. Then George Ballard came in, whistling a cheery tune. "Done with the phone?" he asked, pointing at it.

"Yes." Jumping to her feet, Melanie ran outside.

When Melanie hurried over, her aunt asked, "What did your dad have to say?"

"He's getting married," Melanie replied, trying not to sound upset, angry, or confused. She was having a hard time with all the emotions that were whirling around inside her.

"Married!" Ashleigh sounded as surprised as Melanie felt. "That was sudden."

"That's what I thought." Melanie took the reins from her.

"Let me give you a leg up," Ashleigh offered. Cupping her hands around Melanie's bent knee, she boosted her onto Trib's back.

When Melanie sat up, Kevin and Ashleigh were staring at her as if waiting for her to say more. She busied herself with fastening the chin strap of her helmet.

"Susan seemed pretty cool," Kevin finally said.

Melanie shrugged. "Yeah. I like her."

Ashleigh put her hand on Melanie's calf. "Are you okay?"

Melanie nodded, but tears brimmed in her eyes, making it obvious that she wasn't okay. "I don't want to talk about it," she choked out.

Turning Trib, she squeezed him into a trot. He started right off, his gait bouncy, and she grabbed his mane to keep from slipping.

Without even looking to see if Kevin was coming, Melanie trotted up the hillside to the woods. She wanted to be alone, but there was no way she could politely tell Kevin to get lost after he'd invited her on the ride.

The woods were cool, but she'd forgotten to put fly spray on Trib, and the deerflies attacked. They landed on his ears and neck, drawing blood. Melanie slapped at them, but then one bit her on the arm. Halting Trib underneath some limbs, she ripped off a leafy branch and swatted at the pony's ears.

"Hey, how about using this before you whip your horse to death?" Kevin said, riding up next to her.

He held out his hand. Through blurred eyes, Melanie saw a packet in his palm. It was a fly-repellent wipe.

"Thanks."

He waited while she opened the packet, unfolded the wipe, and rubbed it on Trib's neck and ears. When she was all done and Kevin still hadn't said anything, she blurted, "So aren't you going to ask me a million questions?"

"Nah. I figure when you feel like talking about it, you will."

"Oh." Leading the way, Melanie headed into the woods. After a few turns she realized they were on the hill overlooking Gardener Farms.

She halted the pony. Down below she could see Mona's big barn, the pastures, the ring, and part of the cross-country course. Three horses were trotting around the ring. One was gray, one chestnut, and the third bay.

14

Sterling, Dakota, and Seabreeze, Melanie thought.

"Looks like the dynamic trio are having their lesson," Kevin said, referring to Katie Garrity, Christina, and Dylan Becker. Katie and Dylan boarded their horses at Mona's. They were Christina, Kevin, and Melanie's friends. "You want to go down and watch?"

"No," Melanie said. "I'd rather hang out on the trails. Why don't we go down to the stream and let the horses drink?" She turned Trib around.

He picked up his pace, thinking they were on the way home. But when Melanie steered him down the other path, he balked. She kicked him with her heels. "Come on, stubborn old thing."

He switched his tail, then started reluctantly down the hill. When they reached the stream, the two horses waded into the foot-deep water. Trib dropped his head and took a few sips while Jasper pawed with his hoof.

Melanie couldn't hold back her tears any longer. Great big sobs escaped from her throat.

"Come on, Mel. It can't be that bad."

"Oh, yes, it can. My dad wants me to come back to New York."

"You mean to live? Forever?"

Melanie nodded.

"Bummer."

"I knew things had to change. I just didn't want to think about it. What am I going to do?" She blew out her breath. "I don't want to live in the city."

"Then you should tell him," Kevin said. "Your dad's a cool guy. He'll understand."

"I wish it were that simple."

"It's not?"

"No, because as much as I love it here, my dad's right. I should live with him. We haven't been a family in a long time. I owe it to him—and myself—to try."

Kevin shook his head as if confused. "I guess. But you know, I wish you could stay. I'm really going to miss you."

Melanie glanced shyly at him. "You are?"

His cheeks reddened, and he looked down at his hands resting on Jasper's withers. "Yeah."

Just then Trib bent his front legs and knelt in the water. Melanie screeched as she slid down his neck, plunging into the stream.

With a splash, Trib went all the way down. Kicking up his legs, he rolled sideways in the water. Melanie scrambled to her feet and out of the way.

Just as quickly, the pony jumped up and shook like a dog. Water sprayed everywhere. Melanie threw her hands in front of her face. Not that it mattered—she was already soaked.

Kevin was laughing so hard, he was doubled over Jasper's neck.

"What's so funny?"

"You!" He pointed his finger at her.

"Oh, really?" Melanie snatched up Trib's dangling reins. Sloshing through the water, she walked over to

Jasper. Without a word, she grabbed Kevin's ankle and yanked.

He slipped right off, tumbling sideways into the water. Spitting and sputtering, he stood up. "Hey, no fair. It wasn't my fault Trib rolled."

"You're right," Melanie shot back. "But you could have been sympathetic."

They glared at each other for a second, then started laughing.

"At least I'm not hot anymore," Kevin said.

"And Trib won't need a bath."

"*And* you forgot how gloomy you were," Kevin pointed out as he led Jasper from the water.

But he was wrong, Melanie thought as she followed him, her feet squishing in her sneakers. Taking off her helmet, she shook out the water, then dried the velvet cover on the only spot on her shirt that wasn't wet. "We'd better get home and change clothes," she said. *Home*. When had she started thinking of Whitebrook as home? Not that it mattered. It wouldn't be home for much longer.

Melanie had just finished emptying the dishwasher, and her aunt was standing at the sink, peeling potatoes. Nearby, Christina was setting the table and staring at her cousin.

"What's wrong?" Christina asked, her gaze darting from her mother to Melanie. "Am I missing something? Why do you look so upset, Melanie?"

17

Melanie hadn't meant to keep the news a secret. She just hadn't gotten around to telling Christina about it yet.

"My dad's getting married," Melanie said.

Christina's green eyes widened. "What? You mean to Susan? Why didn't they say anything about it when they were here? When's the wedding?"

"They didn't decide until they left," Melanie explained. "And the wedding is this Sunday."

Christina's mouth dropped open. "Wow, that's in six days!" As if in a daze, she dropped into one of the kitchen chairs. "Wow," she repeated. "Did you have a clue?"

Melanie shook her head. Picking up the silverware, she silently finished Christina's job.

"Her father's calling tonight," Ashleigh explained. "We should know a few more details then."

Melanie must have looked miserable, because Christina said, "You don't look too happy about it, Mel."

"That's because my dad wants me to go back to New York," Melanie said glumly.

"I thought you were going to school with me," Christina said.

"We never decided that, Chris." Drying her hands on a towel, Ashleigh turned away from the sink. "Actually, we never discussed it. The summer went so fast, the subject never came up. I'm afraid that's my fault."

"And mine," Melanie admitted. "I didn't want to talk about school."

"Who does?" Christina said, adding, "And who says you have to go back to New York? I know you love it here. Just tell your dad. He'll understand."

"Kevin said that, too," Melanie murmured. Maybe Christina and Kevin were right—her dad would understand. Tonight, when he called, she'd just tell him the truth: Even though she loved him more than anything, she wanted to stay at Whitebrook.

A hopeful smile spread over Melanie's face. "I'll write down a whole list of reasons why I should stay here—the schools are better, I've made friends, I won't get in trouble . . ."

"Trib and Pirate would miss you," Christina chimed in.

"That's right!" Melanie had been so caught up in her own feelings, she'd forgotten about Pirate. Trib wouldn't care if she ever rode him again—well, maybe he'd miss the treats—but Pirate really counted on her. When she'd come back from Camp Saddlebrook, all the stable hands told her how listless he'd been while she was gone.

Yes, she definitely needed a list in order to convince her dad. Melanie went over to the refrigerator. Pulling off the magnetic pad of paper and pencil that was used for making grocery lists, she began writing as she talked out loud. "One, I can't leave Pirate. Two, Trib would get too fat. Three, Christina would go on a starvation diet."

Looking up at her cousin, Melanie giggled. "Right? You'd stop eating because you missed me so much."

"Sure I'd stop eating—except for pizza, ice cream, and blueberry muffins." Christina laughed, too, but then Melanie glanced at her aunt. Ashleigh was leaning back against the sink. Her arms were folded across her chest and she was frowning.

Melanie's heart sank to her feet. From the look on Ashleigh's face, Melanie knew what her aunt must be thinking—staying wasn't even an option.

3

"NO, THOSE ARE STUPID REASONS FOR WANTING TO STAY here," Melanie blurted. Ripping the sheet of paper off the pad, she crumpled it in her fist.

Christina jumped up from the kitchen chair. "What are you doing? That was a brilliant idea. Dads love lists."

Biting her lip, Melanie peered hesitantly at Ashleigh. Her aunt wasn't frowning anymore, but she was staring at Melanie as if puzzled. "Melanie, before we discuss anything with your dad, you're going to have to decide what you want to do."

"It's not just me who has to make up my mind," Melanie replied, her voice quivering. "You and Uncle Mike have to want me to stay. I wouldn't blame you if you felt I should go back to New York. Two twelve-year-old girls in one house would drive anybody crazy."

21

Ashleigh's brown eyes widened. "Melanie, of course we want you. Whatever gave you the idea we didn't?"

A single tear trickled down Melanie's cheek. "You looked so serious when I mentioned staying, so I thought . . ." Her voice trailed off.

Ashleigh came over and gently put her arm around Melanie's shoulder. "I *was* serious, because it's a big decision, Mel. And your dad should have a say in it, too. Besides—" She hesitated, then frowned again.

"What?"

"In order for you to live here and go to school with Christina, Mike and I would have to become your guardians. That means your father would have to legally sign over his rights as a parent to us."

Melanie snapped her head around. "That sounds awful!"

"I know. And I think your father will feel the same."

"Why can't she just pretend to be my long-lost sister or something?" Christina asked.

"Because we would be legally responsible for her," Ashleigh explained. "We'd have to sign her medical forms and school records, and we'd need proof that she lives in the school district."

"That's dumb," Christina complained.

Melanie exhaled loudly. "Oh, man, why can't this be simple?"

"Because life isn't simple." Ashleigh patted her shoulder, then went back over to the sink. "Think about it while we finish fixing dinner, then discuss it with your dad tonight. You don't want to make a hasty decision."

"You mean like deciding to get married in a week?" Melanie muttered, suddenly angry at her father. It was all his fault, and tonight when he called, she was going to tell him.

"Can I make some brownies, Mom?" Christina asked. "For later, when Dylan and Kevin are here." The boys were coming over after dinner to watch a video.

"Sure. Your father loves brownies, too. Melanie, would you fix a salad?"

"Yeah, fine." Melanie knew they'd already forgotten about her dilemma. Not that she blamed them. After all, the whole thing was *her* problem.

Opening the refrigerator door, she pulled out lettuce, carrots, a cucumber, and a pepper. Ashleigh put a bowl and knife on the counter, and Melanie started tearing off lettuce leaves.

As she fixed the salad she thought about the last time she'd been in New York. Milky Way, the horse she'd been riding at Clarebrook Stables, had been killed in a horrible accident. It had been partly Melanie's fault, but she'd taken all the blame, even though her best friend, Aynslee, had been guilty, too.

Obviously there had been no farewell party when Melanie had left New York. Now, if she went back, everything would be different—so different, she couldn't imagine what it would be like. Would Aynslee even speak to her? Would she be allowed to ride at Clarebrook? Would she be happy?

And what about Pirate? She didn't know anyone at Whitebrook who was interested in riding and caring for a blind ex-racehorse.

A tear rolled down Melanie's cheek and splattered in the salad bowl. *I've got to explain it to Dad*, she told herself as she sliced the cucumber on top of the lettuce. Tonight, when he called, she'd make him understand that no matter how much she loved him, she had to stay at Whitebrook.

Melanie stuck the last hoop in her ear, then inspected her image in the mirror.

She almost didn't recognize herself.

After dinner she'd tinted her hair with green Kool-Aid. Scrounging in her closet, she'd found a denim miniskirt and knit top. Then she'd dug out several pairs of earrings and bracelets. It had been several weeks since she'd dressed like she used to, and the effect was, well, *strange*.

But if she was going back to New York, she'd better practice.

When she walked into the family room, Kevin and Dylan, who were sitting on the overstuffed sofa, did double takes.

"Hey, a Christmas tree," Kevin said.

Melanie didn't laugh. "Thanks for the compliment."

Christina came in carrying a plate of brownies. Jumping off the sofa, Kevin grabbed one and stuffed it in his mouth.

"Great brownies," he mumbled, sitting back down.

"Thanks! I didn't even use a mix," Christina said, holding out the plate to Melanie.

Melanie took one and perched on the armrest of the sofa, next to Kevin.

Putting his hands behind his head, he studied her for a moment. "You look like you did when you first came here."

"You mean like a Christmas tree?"

"No. I was joking. But you look different than you have lately."

"That's because I'm practicing to be a New Yorker again," she said.

"I thought you were gonna tell your father you want to stay here," Kevin said.

"I am. I even made a list." She patted the pocket of her jean skirt. "Christina and Ashleigh helped me. Only I'm not sure it will do any good. You know parents."

"Do I ever. When my sister Samantha decided to live in Ireland, I thought my mom and dad were going to have heart attacks. And she's a lot older than you."

"Why did she leave?"

"She and her husband went over to manage a horse farm there. We haven't seen her in over a year."

Ashleigh stuck her head through the doorway. "Mel? It's your dad. You can use the phone in the office."

Melanie jumped off the arm of the couch. Heart racing, she hurried from the family room. Behind her, Kevin called, "Good luck."

When she reached the office, Melanie took a deep breath, then let it out slowly. Her hands were shaking when she picked up the receiver. "Hi, Dad! Still like the idea of getting married?"

Her father laughed. "Believe me, after being a bachelor for a decade, I don't take getting married lightly. So did you get a chance to think things over?"

"Yes!" Melanie said with forced cheerfulness. "And I've decided I'd rather stay here." Before her father had a chance to respond, she launched into an explanation of how he would have to sign over her guardianship.

When she was through, there was a long silence.

"So what do you think?" she asked.

"I understand what you're saying, Melanie. But there is no way I am giving guardianship to your aunt and uncle."

Melanie bit her lip.

"I know you love it at Whitebrook. But I also remember how much you hated leaving New York. That means I know you can love the city again."

"But, Dad," Melanie protested, "it won't be the same. I probably won't even be able to ride at Clarebrook again."

"Sure you will. Melanie"—his tone changed, and Melanie could hear the wistful hope in his words—"this is our chance to start over. After your mother died,

I tried to be a good parent. But between my growing business and just not knowing the right thing to do, I feel like I let you down. I want to try again. *We* need to try again. Please."

Melanie swallowed the sob in her throat. She nodded even though she knew her father couldn't see her. "You're right, Dad."

"Good. You don't know how happy that makes me." His voice cracked with emotion, and Melanie realized how important it was to him.

"And, Dad, I *am* happy you're getting married. Really."

"Thanks, Melanie. And I'm happy and proud you're my daughter. I've already called about plane schedules. There's a flight to New York on Friday morning. You know, Mel, it's not like you're leaving Whitebrook forever. We can visit every holiday until your aunt and uncle get sick of us."

"Right." Melanie tried to sound enthusiastic.

"Let me speak to Ashleigh again. I want to talk to her about the wedding plans."

"Sure." Melanie covered up the phone and hollered, "Aunt Ashleigh! My dad wants to talk to you."

"I'll get it in the kitchen," she heard her aunt call back.

Slowly Melanie replaced the receiver, then walked into the hall. Closing the door behind her, she stopped and leaned against it.

In the family room, Kevin, Dylan, and Christina

were talking about some of the eighth-grade teachers at Henry Clay Middle School. From the kitchen, she heard Ashleigh exclaim, "*How* many people?"

Pulling the list from her pocket, Melanie unfolded it. *Number one*, it read, *Pirate will miss me.*

Tears filled her eyes. She ripped the list into pieces. Then, shoving them into her pocket, she fled upstairs to her room.

The decision had been made. Friday morning her life would be turned upside down.

MELANIE USED THE SOFT BRUSH ON PIRATE'S BLACK COAT until it shone as brightly as the stars in the night sky. It was early Thursday morning, and she was getting him ready to pony horses.

Stepping back, she surveyed her work. Pirate turned his head in her direction. Even though he couldn't see her, he knew exactly where she was every second.

"You are so-o-o-o handsome," Melanie complimented him, trying to hold back tears. Ever since she'd spoken to her dad, Melanie had been crying on and off. She still couldn't believe she was leaving.

Oh, stop being so gloomy, Melanie scolded herself. She had one more full day at Whitebrook, and she'd made a vow to enjoy every minute.

"Talking to that horse again?" Kevin asked as he

walked down the aisle leading a gangly yearling wearing an exercise saddle.

"He's a good listener. Who's that you're working with?" There were so many young horses at the farm, Melanie knew only a few of them by name. She did know that every Thoroughbred officially turned one year old on January 1, following its birth. From the size of this colt, Melanie figured he was about one and a half years old.

"This is Will O' Wind, nicknamed Willy," Kevin replied, halting the colt about ten feet from Pirate. The colt was too busy chewing on his bit to pay the older horse much attention. "Willy's getting used to being tacked up. Tomorrow Naomi will belly him."

"Belly him?"

"That's when she lies across the saddle on her stomach so he can get used to her weight. Until he's dead quiet, she won't mount all the way."

"That sounds like fun. Do you think I could do that?"

"It's not easy. Sometimes the yearlings get spooked, rear, and fall over backward. You've got to be able to move fast."

Willy danced sideways, banging his flank into the wall. Startled, he jumped forward, almost treading on Kevin's toes. "I'd better get a move on. See you at the track. I hear Naomi, Anna, and Ashleigh are having a practice race."

"I'd love to watch Ashleigh race." Melanie had

only seen her aunt jog horses around the track.

"She's good." Turning the colt, Kevin led him from the barn. As Melanie went into the tack room to get Pirate's saddle and bridle, a wave of sadness washed over her.

There was so much she didn't know about horses. The list was endless. For the past month she'd been working with Terry, a weanling Ashleigh had assigned her to take care of. Handling the six-month-old had taught her a lot about groundwork. If she left Whitebrook now, she'd miss out on so much. Even though her dad had said she'd probably be able to ride at Clarebrook again, Melanie doubted it. Why would they let someone they thought was a horse killer back in the stable?

"Ready to bring me luck this morning?" Naomi asked when Melanie came out of the tack room. The exercise rider was striding down the aisle, a saddle draped over one arm, a crop in her hand. She wore her helmet, leather chaps, and paddock boots.

"I'm afraid I'm all out of luck," Melanie said, unsnapping Pirate's crossties.

"Sorry to hear you're leaving tomorrow. I figured this fall you'd be exercising a few horses on your own."

Melanie's eyes grew round. "Are you serious?"

"Why not? You've got the build. And you can stick on Trib no matter how bratty he's acting. You might be a natural."

"Thanks for the compliment," Melanie said, her

excitement dimming. "But I'm afraid there aren't too many racehorses in Central Park." She draped the reins over Pirate's neck, and he lowered his head to take the bit. When she'd finished tacking him up, she walked him outside, halting in front of the doorway.

A heavy fog hung over the track and pastures. The morning sun was rising, and the farm was bathed in a misty glow.

All across the stable area people and horses moved through the fog like ghosts in a dream. Kevin was leading Willy, Anna Simms was mounting a big gray, Ashleigh rode a big-boned bay toward the track, and Joe Kisner, one of the grooms, held Leap of Faith while Naomi saddled her.

This is my last morning, Melanie thought sadly. *After today I'll never be part of the farm again.* Sure, her dad had promised lots of visits. But visits wouldn't be the same.

When Naomi saw Melanie, she waved her over.

"Let's hope we still bring her luck," Melanie told Pirate. He laid his head on her shoulder. The air was so damp, his coat was covered with fine droplets. For a second Melanie traced his white star with her finger, then ruffled his mane. "Come on, let's get to work."

Joe Kisner came over. "Naomi's ready. Need a leg up?"

"Thanks." Linking his fingers under her knee, Joe boosted Melanie into the saddle. Instantly Pirate quivered with excitement, ready to go.

Melanie found her stirrups, then squeezed her legs against Pirate's sides to signal him to walk. Naomi was

32

turning Faith in a circle, trying to keep her calm. The filly's neck was arched, and she tossed her head nervously. When she saw Pirate she whinnied a greeting, then broke into a jig.

"She's going to miss you guys," Naomi said.

"Won't someone else use Pirate as a pony horse?" Melanie asked as she hooked the lead onto Faith's bit and started toward the training oval.

Naomi gave a small shrug. She was perched high on the exercise saddle, her legs sharply angled. "I doubt it. Kevin ponies sometimes, but he uses Jasper. We've gotten spoiled having you two around. At least I'm spoiled. Faith likes having Pirate beside her. He gives her confidence."

"Who's Ashleigh riding?" Melanie asked, changing the subject before she started to feel bad again. The fog was lifting, and she could see Ashleigh cantering the bay around the oval.

"King Sunday. He's one of Harry Pence's colts, and he's fast. Faith will have her work cut out for her."

Melanie flashed her a smile. "She can do it."

At the gap she unsnapped the lead. Before Faith jogged off, Melanie and Naomi slapped palms for luck.

On the other side of the track the starting gate had been set up. Naomi warmed up Faith at a trot, then a canter. Ian and Maureen Alegretti, his assistant trainer, were by the gate with Ashleigh and Anna. They were helping to load the horses.

"Remember the first day I met you?" Melanie asked

Pirate. "Ian was trying to load you in the starting gate."

In fact, Ian had spent over an hour patiently trying to get the big horse to walk in. He'd been about to give up when Melanie offered to try. Even from the beginning, she'd sensed that Pirate trusted her. And she'd been right. He'd walked into the narrow area without hesitation the first time she led him.

Since then she'd been his only rider and groom. Tomorrow morning, when she said good-bye, it was going to feel terrible.

The slam of the metal doors of the starting gate broke into Melanie's thoughts. Pirate pawed the ground. Even though he hadn't been in many races, he knew what the sound meant.

On the rail about fifty feet from Melanie, Mike stood with a stopwatch in his hand. Finally the three horses were loaded. The bell rang, the doors sprang open, and the three horses leaped from the gate. Dirt flew and hooves pounded as they raced neck and neck around the track.

Slowly Ashleigh and King Sunday inched ahead. Ashleigh rode so smoothly, she and her horse looked like one. *They're going to win,* Melanie thought, but then she saw Naomi hunker low on Faith's neck, lift her hands, and urge her horse with her entire body.

Faith flicked one ear back as if listening to Naomi, then stretched out, her long stride eating the distance between her and King Sunday. With a burst of speed she flew past him, crossing the finish line a length ahead.

"Yes!" Mike hollered.

"All right!" Melanie pumped her fist in the air. Mike had bought Faith on a hunch when she was a scrawny two-year-old. Now, as a three-year-old, she was coming into her own.

Naomi was beaming when she cantered past in the opposite direction, slowly letting Faith wind down. Melanie gave her a thumbs-up sign, and Pirate nickered.

Melanie stroked his satiny neck. "You knew they won, too, didn't you?"

"Mel!" someone called behind her. Melanie twisted in the saddle. Christina was coming up the path to the track. She wore shorts and sneakers, so Melanie didn't think she was heading out for a lesson.

"Morning, Christina," Melanie greeted her. Christina approached Pirate from the side, talking to him so he'd know she was there. "You just missed Naomi and Faith tromping your mom."

"I hope you mean in a race," Christina said. "Hey, big guy." She let Pirate sniff her hand, then scratched under his forelock.

Melanie giggled. "Yes, I mean in a race. Where are you headed?"

"To see you. Mona wants you to come for a lesson this afternoon so the kids at the stable can say good-bye."

"Sounds like a good idea. I'll trot a few pounds off Trib before I leave." She sighed. "I'm going to miss the brat. He taught me a lot about riding, especially jumping."

"He's going to miss you, too." Christina quit scratching Pirate and looked up at her.

"Trib? No way."

Christina nodded. "Don't let the grouch fool you. He went great for you—almost better than he did for me," she added grudgingly.

Melanie grinned. "That's because we're both devious rascals."

"You said it, not me," Christina said, laughing, and Melanie realized for the hundredth time how much she was going to miss her cousin.

And for the hundredth time she told herself not to dwell on it. She could be gloomy after she said her final good-byes tomorrow. Today she was going to stay cheerful—no matter what.

"The place looks deserted," Melanie told Christina that afternoon as the two girls rode up the drive to Mona's. Melanie was on Trib. Christina was riding her horse, Sterling Dream. The Thoroughbred mare was gorgeous—fine-boned and muscular, her black mane and tail accenting her silvery dappled coat.

"I wonder where everybody is." Christina glanced around. They'd taken the shortcut to Gardener Farm, riding along the road instead of through the woods, to make sure they got to Mona's on time for the lesson.

Standing in her stirrups, Melanie craned her neck,

trying to spot someone in the riding ring. "Usually Dylan and Katie are warming up."

"Oh, wait!" Christina smacked the top of her helmet with her palm. "Mona said to come into the office first. She wants to show the video she took at the River Oaks event."

Plopping back into the saddle, Melanie groaned. "Is she trying to torture us?"

"It's not *that* bad," Christina said, pretending to be offended.

When they reached the barn, the girls dismounted and ran up their stirrups.

"Mona said to take off the bridles and put the horses in any empty stall," Christina said as she led Sterling into the barn.

"What if Trib lies down with his saddle on?" Melanie asked, halting the pony in the aisle.

"That does sound like something he'd do." Christina thought a minute. "I guess you'd better untack him completely."

"That's too much work. Why don't I just hold him? I don't really need to watch—"

"No, you're watching," Christina insisted. Dragging Sterling over to Trib, she lifted the flap of Melanie's saddle and unbuckled the girth.

Melanie was surprised by her reaction. "You don't have to get huffy. I'll finish untacking him."

Leading him into an empty stall, she took off the bridle and saddle. Immediately Trib circled, snorting at the strange smells. When Melanie shut the door behind her, Christina was coming out of the stall next door, her bridle draped over one shoulder.

"What do I do with this stuff?" Melanie asked, nodding at the saddle in her arms.

"Oh, just set it somewhere," Christina said impatiently. "And hurry up. Mona's probably started the video already."

"Gee, I can't wait," Melanie grumbled, but Christina had already gone into the office, shutting the door behind her.

Melanie blew out a breath. Somehow she hadn't planned on spending her final afternoon at Whitebrook watching a replay of an event she hadn't even ridden in.

Still, she wanted to be with her friends. And if that was what they wanted to do, she did, too.

Bending, she propped her saddle against the wall and laid the bridle on top. Then she went down the aisle and opened the door to Mona's office and tack room.

A chorus of voices yelled, "Surprise!"

Stunned, Melanie stood in the doorway, staring at the crowd of people jammed into Mona's small office—Ashleigh, Mona, Mike, Kevin, Katie, Dylan. All her friends and family were there, standing under a banner that read WE'LL MISS YOU, MEL!

Melanie opened her mouth to say something, but nothing came out. Suddenly the sadness she'd been trying to squelch all day rose into her chest. Covering her face with her hands, she burst into tears.

5

CHRISTINA RUSHED UP TO HER. "THIS WASN'T SUPPOSED TO make you cry!"

"I know," Melanie choked out. She felt so silly, sobbing like a baby in front of everybody. But she couldn't help it. She was going to miss them like crazy.

"Go ahead and cry," Mike said as he, Ashleigh, and Kevin came up to her. Her uncle put an arm around her shoulder.

"Really? Then you won't be able to eat any cake. Can I have your piece?" Kevin asked, his expression so earnest that Melanie started laughing.

Hastily she wiped her tears away with her fingers. "No. In fact, I'm going to eat ten pieces."

"You're braver than I am." He lowered his voice. "Christina made it."

"Hey!" Christina swatted at Kevin, but he ducked

out of her way and headed for the cake.

Melanie scanned the crowd, spotting Beth McLean, Kevin's mom, Anna and Naomi from Whitebrook, Matt and Sarah, who worked for Mona, and Chad Walker, Katie's boyfriend.

"I hope we didn't miss anybody," Ashleigh said. "We didn't have much time to plan it."

"You did a great job." Melanie felt overwhelmed. No one had ever done anything like this for her before.

"We have good news," Mike said. "We'll be flying out with you in the morning, so you won't be alone."

"That's great!" Melanie flung her arms around her uncle. Just as quickly she stepped away, embarrassed by her emotions.

"After dinner we'll all have to pack," Ashleigh said, then she gave a small shake of her head. "It certainly is sudden."

Melanie laughed. "My father calls it being spontaneous."

"Here's your cake." Kevin handed her a small plate. Christina's creation was vanilla with chocolate icing.

"Yum, my favorite." Then Melanie noticed that Kevin's piece was twice as big as hers. "Pig," she told him as he shoveled in another forkful.

"It's delicious," he mumbled between bites. "I'm getting another piece." When he left, Melanie took a bite. It *was* delicious. She'd have to remember to tell Christina. She looked for her cousin, noticing Cassidy Smith standing in the corner talking to Mona. Cassidy boarded her horses at Mona's, but since she traveled to A-rated shows, she hadn't been around much the past few weeks.

Melanie caught the other girl's eye and waved. "Hey, Cass!" she greeted as she joined them.

"Hi, girl!" Cassidy was tall and slender, with blond hair as sleek and smooth as a model's. "I hear you're leaving us."

"Tomorrow. I'm glad I got to see you before I left. When did you get back from the show?"

"We rolled in early last night. I was pooped. I slept until noon."

"Wow. I haven't done that since I left New York City. How did Welly and Rebound do?" Melanie asked, referring to Cassidy's two horses, a green hunter and a junior jumper.

"She brought back a wheelbarrowful of trophies and ribbons," Mona said.

"Cool." Cassidy traveled all over the East Coast to the biggest shows. The talented rider was earning points for area awards. Still, whenever she got back, she always acted nonchalant about her many wins. "I'd love to watch one of your classes someday," Melanie added.

"Saturday I'm showing in northern New Jersey. Since you and the Reeses are going to be in New York, maybe you could come see me."

"Hey, that sounds great!" Melanie's spirits lifted. With the Reeses in New York and Cassidy right next

41

door, maybe the weekend would turn out okay.

"May I have your attention, please?" Christina announced. She was standing on Mona's desk chair. After she hollered a few more times, the group finally got quiet.

Uh-oh. Melanie wanted to shrink into a corner. Stepping back against the wall, she set her plate on a tack box. She hoped Christina wasn't going to say something that would make her cry again.

"We have an announcement to make," Christina said, grinning at her parents, then at Melanie. "We've really enjoyed having Melanie stay with us, even though she used up all the Kool-Aid and hot water. We also knew how much she'd miss us when she goes back to New York, so we decided to give her a present that will remind her of us every day."

A present? Melanie glanced around. She noticed that Kevin was gone. When she heard the tack room door open, she turned, half expecting to see him coming in with a wrapped package. Instead he was leading Trib through the doorway.

"Kevin!" Mona exclaimed. "Why are you bringing that pony in here?"

"He's Melanie's present."

He led Trib over to her. Speechless, Melanie stared at the pony, then up at Christina and over to Mike and Ashleigh.

"We want you to take him to New York, Mel," Ashleigh said. "All of us agreed that you and Trib really hit it off. Your dad's made arrangements for him to stay at Clarebrook, so you can continue your lessons."

"That means the next time we visit, we expect to see you winning a pony hunter class!" Christina added.

Melanie could only shake her head. "But I—he's—"

"Not yours to keep forever," Mike clarified. "Just until you grow out of him and get your own horse."

"I—I—" Melanie continued to stammer. Then she gave up. Throwing her arms first around Ashleigh, then Mike, she gave them a hug. "Thank you."

Suddenly everybody started to laugh. Melanie drew back, red-faced. But no one was laughing at her. Trib had stuck his nose into her cake, and icing was plastered on his nostrils. Trying to get it off, he was tossing his head and wiggling his lips.

"Oh, Trib!" Melanie exclaimed. "You are such a mess." Then she buried her face in his mane and laughed until she cried.

"This will work out perfectly," Mike said Friday morning. He, Melanie, and Joe Kisner were standing around Whitebrook's horse van. Melanie was holding Trib. He was wearing shipping boots and a lightweight blanket.

Last night, after the party, everyone had packed in a whirlwind of activity. Before breakfast Melanie had put a few last things in her suitcase, then closed it up. She was ready to go.

"You can drop Trib off in New York on Saturday

morning, sleep a few hours, then meet me in the afternoon," Mike told Joe. "I'm checking out some broodmares at a big farm in New Jersey. There's a good chance I'll buy one, and you can bring her home."

"Is the farm in northern New Jersey?" Melanie asked.

"Yes. Why?"

"Maybe you can take Christina and me to a horse show."

"Might be able to. All right, let's get Trib loaded." He took the lead line from Melanie. Trib went willingly up the ramp, but after he'd backed into one of the narrow stalls, he bellowed shrilly, as if realizing what was happening.

"Don't worry, Trib," Melanie called as Mike hooked his halter to the chains. "It'll be all right."

I hope. New York was a long way. Joe was driving all day and part of the night so that Trib would arrive at Clarebrook Stables Saturday morning.

"I'll be there to meet you. With carrots," she promised. Then Joe and Mike lifted the ramp and she couldn't see the pony anymore.

Trib bellowed again. It sounded so sorrowful, Melanie's insides tightened. Trib didn't want to leave Whitebrook, either. She hoped taking him to New York wasn't a mistake.

Turning, she went back into the barn. Sterling had her head over the stall door, a hunk of hay dangling from her mouth. She was staring intently down the aisle, listening to her buddy's calls. Throwing her head up, she whinnied loudly, then listened again. But the roar of the van's motor drowned out Trib's answering cry.

Sterling shook her head, her mane flying, then began to kick the front of her stall door. Trib had been her pasture buddy ever since she'd been at Whitebrook. Melanie knew the mare was going to miss him.

"Just like I'll miss Christina and Kevin and, well, everybody," Melanie said, patting Sterling's silky neck.

She checked the tack room one last time, making sure she hadn't forgotten anything. Christina had helped her pack her helmet, boots, saddle, Trib's bridle, and the horse's brushes in an old trunk, which was headed to New York in the van with Trib. Her chaps and breeches were in her suitcase.

"There you are," Kevin said, peering into the tack room. "Did Trib get off okay?"

"With much protesting." Melanie shoved her hands in the back pockets of her jeans.

"He'll feel better once you take him to a show on Broadway," Kevin joked.

Melanie laughed, but it sounded hollow. She had no idea how to say good-bye to Kevin. When she stepped into the aisle she realized he was feeling just as awkward. His smile was unsure, and a flush was creeping up his neck.

"I don't know what to say, Mel. 'Bye, it's been fun'?"

She shrugged. "Don't say anything. Just promise

that when I come back to visit, it'll be like I was never gone."

"Okay." He grinned shyly. "I've got a present for you."

"You do?"

Whipping his hand from behind his back, he held out a baseball cap. Melanie touched the brim. "It's your Blue Jays cap!"

"Yeah. My mom washed it, so all the sweat rings and grass stains are gone."

Melanie took it and put it on. She knew how much the cap meant to Kevin. Reaching up, he slid it around backward. "I want you to wear it every day to remind yourself that you can still be the Melanie I know—even in New York," he said. Then, ducking his head, he kissed her. Melanie held her breath, feeling his lips brush hers ever so gently.

When he straightened, his face was beet red. "I hope that means you'll write me," Melanie said, blushing slightly herself.

"Are you crazy? My English teachers have been trying to get me to write for years. But I'll call. And next time Mike or my dad goes up to Belmont, I'll visit. You can show me the Big Apple." He took her hand, and they walked to the end of the barn. "Well, I'd better get back to work."

"And I'd better get down to the house. We leave in a few minutes."

"Yeah." He stared at his sneakers.

"Good-bye, Kevin." Melanie squeezed his fingers, then raced from the barn. Good-byes were too hard. She should know. Last night and this morning she'd said good-bye to everybody. Well, almost everybody.

There was still Pirate.

He was standing by the gate in his turnout pasture. Melanie knew he was waiting to be led into the barn for his normal routine. Only this morning things wouldn't be normal at all. She was leaving.

"You get to rest this weekend," she told him, running her fingers down his muzzle. "In fact, you get to rest until I visit again. Kevin will ride you once in a while. And Naomi said she'd bring you treats, and Christina promised to brush you."

Pricking his ears, he pushed at the gate.

"I know you don't understand," Melanie said. "I'm not sure I do, either."

"Mel! It's time to leave!" Ashleigh hollered from the front porch of the house. Christina was climbing into the car, and Mike was putting the last suitcase into the trunk.

Reaching over the fence, Melanie scratched under his mane. At least the others knew why she was going. Pirate would think she'd abandoned him.

"I'll see you soon. *Promise*," she said fiercely, her voice breaking. She gave him a final kiss on the nose, then turned and ran to the car.

She ducked into the backseat, slamming the door behind her. Christina glanced at her but didn't say anything.

When Ashleigh got in the front seat, Mike started the car. "We've got plenty of time to check in, then grab some breakfast before the plane leaves," he told everybody.

Melanie pressed her forehead against the window glass. Pirate was still standing at the gate, gazing in her direction. Melanie knew that even though he couldn't see her, he realized she'd gone away.

He just didn't know how far away she was actually going.

6

MELANIE HAD FORGOTTEN HOW GRAY NEW YORK WAS—gray buildings, gray sky, gray streets, gray sidewalks. Even the people were gray, their faces and clothes blending into the rest of the city.

"Look! There's Rockefeller Center," Christina said excitedly as the cab crept down the busy street. "Do you think we'll have time to sightsee?"

"Not if you girls are going to a horse show Saturday," Mike said from the front seat. Melanie was in the back, squashed between Christina and Ashleigh.

"It's no fair that you guys are running out tomorrow," Ashleigh complained, "instead of helping me decorate the house."

"We can help tonight," Melanie said. "I think toilet paper streamers would be simply divine."

Christina laughed. "Strings of popcorn would be a classy touch, too."

"And shaving cream swirls on the walls," Mike added.

Ashleigh rolled her eyes. "Very funny, guys. I guess it's better you won't be helping."

"With Susan so hyper about everything, I don't want to be around her until after the wedding," Melanie grumbled. Her dad and Susan had called every night of the past week with different plans.

Ashleigh sighed. "I know what you mean. Actually, I'm going to try to escape tomorrow afternoon and visit Cindy at Belmont."

Cindy McLean, Ian and Beth's adopted daughter, was a jockey. Melanie had never met Cindy, who'd been living in New York State for the past several years.

"No fair!" Christina exclaimed, sitting forward to peer at her mother around Melanie. "I want to see Cindy, too."

"Good. Melanie can go to the show while you help me fold napkins and make hors d'oeuvres all morning."

"Uh, on second thought, I'll see Cindy another time," Christina murmured.

"We're here," Mike told Melanie.

The cab pulled up in front of the Grahams' three-story brick townhouse. Melanie shifted forward so she could see out the window.

The townhouse was fourth in a long row of homes that had been built in the late 1800s. They had stone steps, ornate iron railings, and fancy detailing. The neighborhood was an exclusive and desirable section of Manhattan close to Central Park, but after living at Whitebrook, all Melanie could think about was how small the homes looked.

"We'll drop you off, then head to our hotel," Mike said. "Tell your dad we'll be over later."

The driver got out of the car and went around to get Melanie's luggage from the trunk. Ashleigh opened the door and climbed out, Melanie's backpack in her hand.

When Melanie hesitated, her aunt bent down and peered in at her. "Coming?" she asked.

Melanie swallowed hard. She was frozen to the seat, afraid to move.

"Hey, Mel, don't worry. The sidewalk won't bite," Christina said gently. "And we'll see you soon—promise."

Melanie smiled ruefully. Those were the same words she'd said to Pirate, yet she had no idea when she would see him again.

"You'd better keep that promise," she told Christina before clambering out.

"Okay, Mel, we'll see you in a little while," Ashleigh said, handing her the backpack. "And smile a little. I bet things won't feel quite so bad once you see your dad." After giving Melanie a hug, she climbed back in.

Melanie watched as the cab inched out into traffic. Through the back window, she could see Christina waving madly.

Lifting her hand, she wiggled her fingers. Then she turned and faced the building. She was surprised that her dad and Susan hadn't rushed out to meet them. Now she had to knock like some stranger.

Flinging her pack over one shoulder, Melanie trudged up the steps and rang the bell. The door flew open, and Susan greeted her with a wide smile.

"Melanie! We didn't hear you drive up!" Taking her pack, Susan ushered her into the hallway. Standing at the foot of the steps, Melanie glanced down the hall, then over her shoulder into the formal living room. Everything looked the same—and yet different.

There were still Oriental rugs on the hardwood floors, and the same beautiful but untouchable antique furniture. Melanie's mother had had excellent taste, and when she'd died, her father had left the main rooms exactly the same. Susan had already made a few changes. The heavy curtains had been replaced by swags that let in streams of light, and on every table was a vase of cut flowers.

"We're so excited to have you back, Melanie," Susan was chattering as she brought in the rest of the luggage from the stoop. "Did you have a good flight?'

"Where's Dad?" Melanie asked.

Susan smiled apologetically. She was dressed casually in white jeans and a scoop-necked T-shirt. Her dark hair was pushed back in a band, making her look twenty instead of forty. "As usual, he's in his office on the phone. He'll be out in a minute. Should we take your things upstairs? Angela's so busy with wedding preparations, I don't dare ask her to help."

Melanie picked up one suitcase. "Sure. I'd like to see my room. I guess it's still my room?" She hesitated on the bottom step.

"Of course. I'm not planning on changing anything without your input, Melanie."

Only you already did, Melanie thought as she clumped up the steps. She knew she wasn't being very friendly, which wasn't fair to Susan. It wasn't Susan's fault Melanie had to move back.

Yes, it was, a voice chirped. If her father weren't getting married, none of this would have happened.

Melanie paused at the top of the stairs. Her room, her dad's, and two baths were on the second floor. On the third floor was a room and bath for Angela, and her mother's art studio, which had been closed up for years. Melanie wondered if Susan had taken that over, too.

Slowly she walked down the hall, stopping to look into the master bedroom. It was as cluttered and messy as always. Obviously Susan hadn't moved in yet.

Melanie shuddered at the thought of sharing the house with a stranger. Even though she liked Susan, liking someone was a lot different from living with someone.

As she walked down to her doorway Melanie's heart started pounding. It seemed stupid to be so nervous about a room, but she'd left in such a hurry after

Milky Way's accident that she hadn't had a chance to put things in order.

The door was open. The room was the same—her purple spread and curtains, the barrage of stuffed animals on the bed and shelves, her desk and computer—only everything was so neat, it looked like a picture in a magazine instead of a real room.

Coming in behind Melanie, Susan set her suitcase on the floor. "Angela gave it a good cleaning, but we didn't touch a thing. Though we did *add* something." Clasping her fingers together, she looked at Melanie, a faint smile on her face.

Melanie turned, her heart flip-flopping when she spotted what Susan was talking about. On the wall beside the door were two framed drawings of Pirate. She recognized them instantly, since she was the one who had drawn them.

"Where'd you get those?" Melanie demanded.

"Christina."

"She stole them from my art pad?"

Susan furrowed her brow. "No. She said you'd given them to her."

"Oh, right. I forgot." Turning her back on the pictures, Melanie tossed her pack on the bed. "Thanks. They look great."

"You're welcome," Susan said, adding in a soft voice, "I'll see if your father's off the phone."

When she left, Melanie dove onto the bed and buried her face in her arms. *Oh, stop being so touchy,* she

54

scolded herself. But everything she saw reminded her of how different things were going to be.

And how rotten she felt.

"Hey, sweetie!" a voice boomed.

Melanie lifted her head. Her father strode into the room, sat on the edge of the mattress, and bounced like a kid. "Need a thrill?" he joked. "Susan says you seem pretty down."

"No. Just a hug." Twisting to a sitting position, Melanie threw herself into her father's arms before he could see her tears.

"It'll be okay," he said, stroking her back. "Just give it a chance."

She nodded, her chin scraping the buttons on his polo shirt. "I know."

"When are Ashleigh, Mike, and Christina coming?"

"They said they'll be here soon."

"Good. Susan and I marinated steaks to grill."

"Grill? You sound positively domestic," Melanie teased.

"Things are going to change. I made a promise to limit client dinners so we could eat together at least three nights a week."

Only three nights? That still meant a lot of pizza with just Angela and the TV for company. At Whitebrook they'd eaten together almost every night, sometimes setting an extra place for Naomi or Joe or one of the many people who worked at the farm.

Oh, stop comparing, Melanie told herself. It wasn't fair.

"And we made three kinds of salad," her father went on. "And—what's your favorite dessert?" Holding her at arm's length, he searched her face as if puzzled. "Was it chocolate-covered ants? Bananas flambé?"

Melanie giggled. "Very funny. You know what it is." Her eyes drifted to the pictures of Pirate on the wall behind her father. "Thanks for the drawings. I know Susan thinks I didn't like them, but seeing Pirate just made me feel so sad."

Her father let out a sigh. "Believe me, if there were any way I could've brought him to New York, I would have. But a blind horse in Central Park would need a Seeing Eye dog."

Melanie laughed in spite of herself. "I know. Besides, Pirate would have been miserable away from the training track. Trib will miss Whitebrook enough."

Her voice must have sounded sad, because her father wrapped his arms around her even tighter, holding her so close Melanie could feel his heart beating.

This is why I'm here, she thought. *Because I love my father so much*. She just had to keep reminding herself of that.

"Hungry?" he asked. Pulling away, Melanie sat on the mattress next to him.

"Starved. All they served on the plane was peanuts. Did Ashleigh tell you that Christina and I are going to New Jersey tomorrow to see a friend of ours compete in a show? We'll leave after Trib gets settled."

He nodded. "That's just as well. Things will be crazy

around here until the wedding's over. By the way, Aynslee called."

Melanie's eyes widened. "She called to talk to me?"

"She wondered if you were coming home in time for school." He chucked her under the chin. "See? Your friends haven't forgotten you. I invited her and Heather to the party. I thought it would be a good way to break the ice—you know, make jokes about your old fossil of a father getting married again."

"Hey, Heather's the one who had a crush on you."

His brows rose. "She did? You'd better not tell Susan. She's the jealous type."

"Yeah, right," Melanie scoffed. "She's the one who's around handsome rock stars all day. An old dinosaur like you should be jealous of *her*."

"Thanks for the compliment." He stood up, the springs creaking. "Why don't you unpack while we finish getting dinner ready?"

"Okay. I'll call Aynslee, too." Melanie watched him leave, then reached for the phone and dialed. She was kind of excited to hear what her old friend had been up to all summer.

"Melanie? Is it really you?" Her friend sounded so excited that Melanie couldn't help but grin. "Are you calling from New York?"

"I am. I heard that Dad invited you to the reception. I hope you and Heather can come. I'd love to see you."

"Of course we're coming. I asked your dad if he'd invited any rock stars. He acted vague, like maybe someone hot was going to be there. Are they? Did he tell you?"

Melanie frowned. "Rock stars? I don't think so. "

"I bet he invited Harvey of the Headknockers. Heather and I bought new duds just in case. Spent a wad of money. We are going to look so cool. We've been trying to guess who might be there. Does your dad know the Rangers?"

"It's going to be a small reception, so I—"

"Yeah. I know what 'small' means in showbiz terms. Small's like a hundred or more. So what are you going to wear? And is the country mouse going to be there?"

"Country mouse" was the old nickname Melanie had given Christina, and she hadn't meant it in a complimentary way, either. Now when she heard Aynslee say the name, it made her bristle.

"Watch it, Ayns. I'm a country mouse now, too."

"Not for long. I bet in a week you'll quit smelling like manure." Aynslee giggled. "I mean, I don't know what you did all summer at that farm. Milk cows? Shovel pig poop? Anyway, you're back in the big city, and that's all that matters. Too bad you weren't here this summer. Heather and I had the coolest time. We've been hanging out with Pete and Robert from Manhattan Prep. They said they missed you."

She rattled on and on, only Melanie had stopped listening. All she could think about was how different Aynslee was from the kids in Kentucky. In fact, she couldn't believe they'd once been best friends. Had she,

Melanie, changed so much that she found every word out of Aynslee's mouth irritating instead of fun?

She hoped Aynslee was just showing off. Her old friend had always been starstruck as well as a bit of a braggart. Before, Melanie had just accepted it as part of Aynslee's quirky personality. Now she wasn't so sure.

The doorbell rang. Still hanging on to the receiver, Melanie jumped up from the bed. Stretching the cord taut, she walked to the front window that overlooked the street.

Below she could see the tops of Ashleigh's and Mike's heads. Between them she spotted Christina's reddish gold hair.

"Aynslee, I've got to go. We've got company."

"Who? Billie and the Heartbreakers? Ruby Two?"

"No. Even more famous than those two groups," Melanie replied, exaggerating dramatically. "I'll tell you and Heather all about them on Sunday."

Aynslee squealed excitedly. After saying good-bye, Melanie dropped the phone back onto the hook and, laughing to herself, ran downstairs to answer the door.

7

CLAREBROOK STABLES WAS LOCATED TWO BLOCKS FROM Central Park and five blocks from Melanie's house. She'd walked the route so many times she could have done it blindfolded.

This time, though, she was so anxious that she kept forgetting where she was. In thirty minutes Trib would be in New York. Joe had called around eight that morning. If traffic wasn't terrible, he and Trib would arrive by nine.

Not that she was worried about seeing Trib. It was going to Clarebrook that was making Melanie's palms sweat and her stomach churn. Her dad had told her the stable had a new manager, which was why she'd been allowed to return so easily. Still, a lot of the old boarders, instructors, and students were there. Would they be angry she was back? Would they give her the cold shoulder?

She knew that she would find it hard to forgive someone who had caused a horse's death. The only person who might forgive her would be Jonathan Kelly, her instructor. He knew how much she cared about horses. He must realize how terrible she felt.

The morning was sunny and warm, and the sidewalks were filled with joggers, dog walkers, in-line skaters, and tourists. Dodging the throngs of people, Melanie crossed the street and made her way to the stable, an old brick two-story building that had once been a livery stable.

As Melanie hurried the last block she couldn't help but compare Clarebrook to Whitebrook. There were no rolling pastures, white board fencing, or wooded hillsides. In fact, the stable was surrounded by parking garages, apartment houses, and honking traffic. Still, if she wanted to ride, it was her only choice.

When she was almost there, she broke into a jog. The Whitebrook van was parked in front. Joe must have made good time.

He was dozing in the driver's seat, the brim of his baseball cap pulled low over his eyes. Melanie knocked on the window of the cab. He jerked awake, then smiled and opened the door when he saw it was her.

"How's Trib?" Melanie asked.

"Tired and cranky. Last time I watered him, he tried to bite me." Jumping from the cab, Joe stretched, then adjusted his cap. "I'm a little worn out myself."

"Did you tell someone in the office you were here?"

He nodded. "Yup. The stall's ready. Should we unload him?"

Melanie nodded eagerly. "Mike and Christina should be here any minute, and I'm sure Trib wants to stretch his legs."

"You just keep a tight hold on him," Joe warned as he walked back to the side of the van. "We don't want him bolting into traffic."

Melanie helped lower the heavy ramp. When light streamed into the back of the van, Trib whinnied shrilly. Then he lunged forward, tugging at the chains hooked to his halter.

"Just a second, Trib," Melanie said. The pony appeared to be fine, but she knew the trip had been hard on him. He'd been standing in one place for almost twenty-four hours.

"Let me get him out," Joe suggested. "He'll be wired."

Wired was right. Ears flicking wildly, the pony peered out the open door. Trib was used to a lot of noise and confusion, but the sounds of the city were a new experience.

Turning to face the street, Melanie pretended she was Trib. What would the city be like to a pony who'd lived on a farm? Colorful cabs and buses clogged the streets, their motors roaring, their brakes squealing. Cyclists and skaters whizzed by, calling to each other, and in the distance she could hear sirens and horns.

It would be noisy and confusing, Melanie decided.

"It'll be all right, Trib, you'll see," she reassured him, but she wasn't too sure herself.

Joe led him down the ramp. Just as Trib got to the bottom an ambulance sped by. He whirled to stare, almost knocking Joe over. Then, spotting a horse and carriage, the pony plunged forward, nickering plaintively.

"Whoa, buddy," Joe crooned. He was used to handling the jumpiest of racehorses, but Trib was managing to give him a hard time.

Melanie knew she'd better not lead him. If he pulled away from her . . . She shook her head, not even wanting to imagine what might happen.

"Let's get him inside," she said, heading to the big garage door where the horses went in and out of the stable.

When Melanie stepped through the wide opening, she halted and looked around. She'd forgotten how dark and tiny the stable was, with an indoor arena half the size of Mona's ring. Since it was Saturday morning, a lesson was going on.

Trib whinnied loudly to the three school horses plodding around the ring. Jonathan Kelly was teaching the class. When he turned to shoot them an exasperated look, she waved hesitantly.

His eyes widened in surprise. He turned back to his students without even smiling at her.

"Where to?" Joe asked.

Melanie pointed to an aisle that led to an office door and a ramp. "Up there."

Joe halted Trib at the bottom of the ramp. "Up there?" he repeated, giving Melanie a puzzled look.

"Yes. It goes to the second floor. Dad paid extra for one of the box stalls." Walking past the office door, she pointed to a ramp that slanted downward. "That leads to the 'dungeon,' where they keep the school horses."

Melanie shivered as she gazed into the dark basement. Milky Way had been stabled in the dungeon, and the last time she'd been down there was the night of the accident.

When she walked past the office she glanced inside. Several riders in breeches and helmets stood around the desk, manned by a young woman. It was Jaylaan, the employee who scheduled the lessons and Central Park rides.

Melanie said hi, then followed Joe and Trib up the ramp. The pony trod carefully on the wooden surface, then scrambled the last few feet. Compared to the dungeon, the upstairs was light and airy, with two rows of box stalls opening onto a center aisle. Walking ahead, Melanie found an index card with Trib's name on it tacked to a stall door.

"In here," she told Joe. The stall was deeply bedded with straw. A wooden feed tub, worn from years of use, hung from one wall. An automatic waterer was in the corner.

"I'll let him inspect his new home. When the lesson's over I'll walk him around the arena if there's time," Melanie said.

Trib followed Joe into the stall. Bars separated each stall, but immediately a horse poked his nose between them to smell his new neighbor. As soon as Joe unhooked Trib he pranced over to the horse, sniffed deeply, and squealed.

Melanie grinned. "At least he found a friend. I wonder who it is." She peered into the stall, realizing it was Brutus, the dun horse Jonathan often rode.

"I'm going to get your trunk, then close up the van," Joe said. "Do I go down the ramp?"

"Yeah. Just watch for horses coming up."

When Joe left she walked slowly down the aisle, breathing in the smells. The stalls were clean, the horses' coats shiny. Stopping in front of a barred window, she gazed outside. A small group of riders was headed down the street toward Central Park. Maybe Clarebrook wasn't Whitebrook, Melanie thought, but at least she would be around horses.

When she got back to Trib's stall, he was licking the feed tub. "Nothing there. Sorry," Melanie said as she went in to take off his blanket and shipping boots.

Gathering them in her arms, Melanie went down to the office to find out what locker she had been assigned. Boarders kept their personal things locked up. The tack and supplies for the school horses were hung on the outside wall of the their stalls.

"Hi, Jaylaan," Melanie greeted the older girl, a senior in high school who worked at the stable on weekends and after school.

Jaylaan gave her a curious look. "I heard you were coming back. Your locker's number *thirteen*."

She said the word so dramatically that Melanie couldn't help but realize what she was implying—thirteen, an unlucky number.

"Thanks." Melanie took the lock in her free hand.

"Next," Jaylaan said without even looking at her.

Well, at least I know what it's going to be like around here, Melanie thought as she went into the tack room. But she knew she could handle it—as long as she got to ride Trib.

Setting the blanket and boots on a long bench, Melanie opened the locker door. It smelled stale and was plastered with dust. She went into the tiny bathroom and found some cleanser. By the time Joe came back, the locker was clean enough to put her stuff in.

When she'd finished unpacking her trunk Joe checked his watch. Melanie knew he was eager to leave. "I wonder what's keeping Christina and Mike," she mused.

"Traffic, probably. If you're okay, I'm going to head out. Mike gave me directions over the phone."

"Mel!" Christina's voice came from outside the tack room, and a second later her cousin bounded in. Melanie grinned, really happy to see her. "It's about time!"

"The traffic was the pits. Dad never did get a parking place. He squeezed in behind the van." Christina turned in a circle, checking out the tack room. "Boy, being at Clarebrook brings back memories," she told Melanie. "Remember what a jerk you were when I first met you? You brought me here to ride and gave me the worst horse—on purpose."

Melanie groaned. "Don't remind me. Do you want to see Trib? He's all settled."

Christina shook her head. "Dad says we need to leave now so he can drop us off and get to the farm in New Jersey before lunch."

"I'm ready." Joe hoisted the empty trunk.

"I guess I am, too." Melanie had already called and told the stable manager about Trib's feed. "Just let me run up and kiss Trib good-bye. He'll think we abandoned him."

"Okay. We'll help Joe close up the van. Meet us outside."

Melanie followed Joe and Christina from the tack room. When she went up the ramp to the second floor, a young woman who looked about twenty was leading a huge chestnut horse down the aisle. She smiled politely. "Welcome to Clarebrook. Is this the first time you've boarded a horse here?" she asked in a German accent.

"Uh, yes," Melanie said truthfully. "What about you?"

"Me too. I just arrived from Germany to spend a semester at Columbia University. I decided to bring Gustav with me to remind me of home." She patted the horse's thick neck. He had big feet, huge cannon bones,

68

and a round, muscular rump. Melanie had never seen such a big horse.

The woman put out her hand to shake Melanie's. "I'm Bettina Krueger. Perhaps we can ride in the park sometime. You can show me the trails."

"I'd love to."

Trib was munching on his hay. Since Melanie could see Brutus on the other side of the bars, she knew that at least the pony wasn't lonely.

Opening the door, she checked him all over, then gave him a pat. "I'll come visit this evening," she promised. "Maybe we can even go for our first ride in the park."

Trib ignored her, his attention on the hay. Melanie was glad he'd settled in so quickly. She shut the stall door, latching it securely, then hurried down the ramp. She wanted to stop at the office and see if Mr. Franco, the new manager, was there, so that she could let him know Trib had arrived.

As she went down the aisle toward the office, several people said hello. Melanie didn't recognize them—which was good, she decided. With so many new people at the stable, things might not be so bad after all. Especially if she could start lessons right away with Jonathan.

She reached the open office door and was about to turn in when she heard someone say, "What is she doing here?"

The words stopped Melanie cold.

"Her dad, Mr. Hotshot Record Producer, convinced Franco to board some pony."

"Does Franco know about the accident?"

"Probably. But he doesn't care. Her father's paying double for a box stall."

Horrified, Melanie flattened herself against the wall. No wonder she'd been allowed to come back to the stable.

"Well, I care. I'm telling Franco she's not to ride one of the school horses. *Ever*."

With a start, Melanie recognized the person's voice. It was Jonathan, and his angry tone told Melanie that things were definitely *not* going to be okay.

8

"DO YOU SEE CASSIDY?" CHRISTINA ASKED MELANIE. SHE was leaning forward, staring out the windshield of the rental car.

"I see about fifty girls wearing identical helmets and hunt coats who might be her," Melanie replied. Rolling down the window, she stuck her head out and let the hot air blow her short hair into whorls.

The show grounds were packed with trailers, vans, and horses. *Gorgeous* horses. So gorgeous they made Melanie drool. She was used to lanky Thoroughbreds that were racing fit. These horses had round, sleek bodies, classical heads, and dainty hooves.

"Gee, I thought Sterling was beautiful," Christina said in a subdued tone. "But these horses are perfect."

"You bought Sterling because you knew she was going to be athletic enough to event," Mike said. "These

71

horses are bred and raised for conformation and smooth, flowing gaits. I'm not sure they could handle a gallop through a stream and then a leap over a liverpool."

Christina punched her dad affectionately on the shoulder. "Thanks. You always know how to make me feel better."

"I'll take that one," Melanie said as they passed a handsome bay. His coat and hooves gleamed, and his star and socks were so white they looked painted on.

"And spend all your time grooming him." Christina laughed.

"What kind of rig does Cassidy have?" Mike asked. "That may be the best way to find her."

"She's with her old instructor—there!" Christina pointed to a modern six-horse trailer with the name "Fairfield Stables" written on the side. Cassidy had just moved to Kentucky, so over the summer she had continued to train and compete with her instructor from Florida.

Pulling to the right of Cassidy's trailer, Mike parked. Melanie and Christina climbed out. Inside the trailer, Rebound, Cassidy's jumper, stood in one of the stalls eating hay from a net.

"She's here," Melanie told Christina. "Rebound's in the trailer."

"Looking for Cass?" a guy about their age asked. He was dressed in show attire and held the reins of a pretty mare with a blaze down her dished face.

"Yes." Melanie stroked the chestnut's velvety neck. "Wow, your horse is gorgeous."

The guy shrugged. "She should be. My dad paid fifty thou for her."

Melanie started to choke. Christina poked her in the side with her elbow. "Shape up, Mel," she hissed. "Most of these horses cost that much."

"Cass and Wellington are jumping next." He jerked his head toward one of the show rings, then led his horse away.

"Fifty thousand dollars?" Melanie repeated.

"This is one of the top shows on the East Coast," Christina explained. "That means the horses have to be flawless."

They walked around to the other side of the van, which faced the show ring. When they spotted Cassidy mounted on Wellington, her handsome gray Thoroughbred, Christina went back to the car to tell Mike that he could leave.

As Melanie waited in the shade of the van, she watched a rider jump the course of eight fences. Christina was right: The horse in the ring was perfect. So perfect, he almost didn't look real—the smooth, relaxed way he leaped every fence, picking up his front legs to exactly the same height, his ears pricked, his neck arched as if he were a robot programmed for a faultless round.

"Dad'll pick us up in a couple of hours," Christina said when she rejoined Melanie.

"This is fascinating," Melanie said. "How do the riders get the horses to canter so evenly and so eagerly? Trib would be charging around with his ears pinned."

"Bribe them?" Christina guessed as she took off for the in-gate. Cassidy was talking to a guy wearing sunglasses. Both of them wore intense expressions. Welly only looked bored.

"That must be her instructor," Christina said.

"Great. Let's say hi."

"Wait." Christina put her hand on Melanie's arm to stop her from going over. "She looks pretty uptight. Let's say hi when she's finished this class."

"Keep Welly collected around the far corner," the guy was saying as he gestured toward the end of the ring, "or he'll get too strung out."

Cassidy was frowning and nodding. Melanie thought she looked elegant in her black velvet hunt cap, navy blue coat with a fine pinstripe, tight white breeches, and high, slender black boots.

Melanie couldn't help but feel envious. Since the first day Cassidy had arrived at Mona's, she'd acted like a cool, composed professional—even though she was only a year older than Melanie and her friends.

Maybe someday I'll be like that, Melanie thought as she followed her cousin to a shady spot along the rail. In front of them was a brush jump flanked by blue-and-white standards. Excited, Melanie leaned on the top rail of the ring and watched the horse finish his round.

She was so entranced by the show, she'd almost forgotten about the incident at the stables. Not that she was planning on telling Christina what Jonathan had said. After tomorrow her cousin wouldn't be around. She'd have to learn to deal with stuff herself.

"Number ninety-two, please enter the ring," the announcer called.

Christina clutched Melanie's arm. "That's Cassidy!"

Melanie held her breath as Cassidy rode Welly into the ring. After cantering a warm-up circle, she headed him toward the first line of fences. The Thoroughbred's pace was so smooth, his strides so even, it was as if he floated around the ring and over the obstacles.

As he approached the brush Melanie pumped her arms, as if she were the one riding him. Beside her, Christina was holding pretend reins and urging the duo on, too. Then Melanie heard the sound of dirt spraying up against the jump, and Welly was over and cantering toward the last line.

When the pair finished, applause burst out.

"Yay!" Christina and Melanie cheered. "Great job, Cass!"

Cassidy must have heard them, because she snapped her head around and stared in their direction before leaving the ring.

"That's gotta be a blue-ribbon round," Melanie said. "Let's congratulate her." Grabbing Christina's wrist, she tugged her cousin toward the exit gate.

Cassidy had dismounted and was running up her stirrups. Her instructor, Mannie, stood beside her, holding Welly. "Well done, Cassidy. You looked fantastic."

"Thanks. But did you notice Welly hesitated before the fence? Maybe there was a shadow or something that spooked him."

"I wouldn't worry about it." He walked off to talk to someone nearby, and the girls approached.

"I thought I heard you guys cheering," Cassidy said, grinning. "I'm so glad you actually made it."

"You did great," Christina said. "Hey, Welly." She scratched the gray under the braid in his forelock. "You look so much like Sterling, you're making me homesick."

"After they pin this class, I'm ready for a break. How's a chili dog with relish and onions sound?"

"Gross," Melanie said.

They hung around the in-gate, waiting for the class to finish and the judges to make their decision. Finally the announcer said, "Will these horses please jog into the ring in this order—number eighty-five, number one-oh-three, number ninety-two . . ."

"That's you!" Melanie thumped her friend on the shoulder.

"Third—not bad." Cassidy shrugged as if it was no big deal, then led Welly into the ring.

"I'd be ecstatic," Christina said. "Especially considering the tough competition."

Ten minutes later Cassidy emerged from the ring, a yellow ribbon fluttering from Welly's brow band. "Here, I'll take him back for you," Melanie offered.

Taking Welly's reins, she led the big gray back to the van. His head was lowered and his ears flopped as if he was exhausted.

"Are you tired of the dust, the noise, and the endless van rides?" Melanie asked him as they plodded along. Trailing behind, Cassidy was telling Christina how many points she'd have to win to get a championship.

When they reached the van, a girl of about fifteen hustled over to take Welly from Melanie. "Is there time to bathe him?" she asked Cassidy.

"Yes. And let him graze for a few minutes. I'm getting some lunch."

Pulling off her helmet, Cassidy dropped it on top of a tack trunk. With a weary groan, she plopped next to it.

"Who's that?" Melanie asked, gesturing to the girl who was untacking Welly.

"Julia. She's Mannie's working student."

"Working student?"

"Yeah. She mucks stalls, grooms, braids—you know, grunt work—in return for lessons. She doesn't own a horse, which is too bad, because she's a good rider."

"She doesn't get to show?" Christina asked.

"Sometimes she gets to ride one of Mannie's green horses. Or she'll catch-ride."

Puzzled, Melanie arched her brows, and Cassidy laughed. "That means she'll ride anybody's horse for a few bucks. Man, it's good you guys came. I can see you need educating."

"Not me," Christina said. "I'm sticking with eventing."

"What about you, Mel?" Cassidy pulled off her boot and sock and, with a sigh, rubbed her foot.

Melanie shrugged. "I don't know what I want to do." Quickly she bent to help pull off Cassidy's other boot. "So, when's your next class?" she asked, changing the subject. She didn't want to have to explain that she probably wouldn't even get to take lessons anymore. Not with the way Jonathan felt about her.

"I jump Rebound after lunch. That gives me about half an hour just to goof." Standing up, she wiggled her toes. "Ah. That feels good."

Taking off her hunt coat, she hung it up in the trailer's dressing room. Then she pulled off her helmet and hair net. When she combed her hair, it fell smoothly into place.

"How come your hair doesn't get all plastered to your head?" Christina asked.

Cassidy winked. "It's well trained, just like my horses."

Laughing, the three girls headed to the concession stand, where they ordered hot dogs, chips, and sodas.

"Love this healthy food," Melanie said as they sat down under a shady tree to eat.

When they were finished, Melanie and Christina helped Cassidy get ready for her jumper class. Rebound was a lot taller than Welly and built more like a race-horse, with sinewy muscles and long legs. Melanie liked his rugged looks better than those of the sleek hunters.

"How high will you be jumping?" Christina asked.

"The obstacles start at three feet six inches," Cassidy explained as she buckled Rebound's girth.

"I thought they'd be higher," Christina said.

"Well, they go as high as five feet for jump-offs," she added. "With spreads as wide as five feet."

Christina's mouth fell open.

"That's as tall as I am," Melanie said. "Aren't you afraid to jump something that huge?"

"I'm afraid I'll knock down a pole or get time penalties, but no, I'm never afraid of jumping."

Melanie was impressed. She remembered her first time over the cross-country course at Camp Saddlebrook. The fences had been tiny, yet she'd been scared to death.

When Cassidy rode Rebound to the warm-up area, Melanie and Christina strolled to the ring to watch the jumper class that had started. Melanie's jaw dropped when she saw the size of the fences. "An elephant wouldn't be able to jump over those."

Christina giggled. "Elephants can't jump, silly."

In silent awe, Melanie watched the riders expertly steer their mounts around the tight course. When Cassidy trotted Rebound into the ring, Melanie knew right away they were going to do well. Cassidy oozed quiet confidence. Her touch was light on the reins as she guided Rebound around the course. Without the slightest hesitation, he effortlessly cleared each fence, his back arched, his legs tucked to his chest.

As they turned, twisted, and flew, an energy radiated from them and into Melanie. *That's what I want to do,* she decided. Maybe one day she'd learn to ride jumpers like Cassidy.

Later, when Uncle Mike picked them up, Melanie was still wired. She and Christina chattered excitedly all the way through New Jersey. It wasn't until they'd crossed the Hudson River that her excitement faded.

As they drove into Manhattan Melanie's spirits sank lower as the buildings grew taller. Tomorrow was the wedding, and then Christina and her family would leave.

Melanie told herself that she could handle it. But the dull pain in her stomach told her it wouldn't be easy.

9

"Christina? Is that you? And wait, no, it can't be Melanie, my daughter!" Will Graham exclaimed with mock astonishment when the two girls came down the steps of the townhouse. "Aren't you the one who usually has blue hair?"

"Dad, you are so corny," Melanie retorted, but secretly she was pleased. It was early Sunday afternoon, and she and Christina had spent an hour dressing. They both wore flower-print dresses with flowing calf-length skirts. Ashleigh had given them each a daisy to tuck behind one ear, and when they begged to wear makeup, she'd let them dab on blusher and lipstick.

"You look strange, too," she added, giving him a hug. "Like a groom instead of a dad."

Even though Susan wasn't wearing a white gown, Will had chosen to wear a formal tux. He'd trimmed his stylishly long hair and removed his earring. Only his neon pink cummerbund reminded Melanie that the person about to get married was her father.

"Did you see Susan?" he asked.

"Yes, but we're not telling you what she's wearing," Christina declared.

"Except that it *is* clothes," Melanie assured him.

He pretended to wipe sweat off his brow. "That's a relief."

The doorbell rang, and Will went to open it. When he ushered the guests in, Melanie recognized several people who worked with her father and Susan.

Melanie tugged on Christina's sleeve. "Come on, let's go into the kitchen and see what there is to eat. I'm starved."

"You mean let's get out of here so we don't have to talk to grown-ups," Christina corrected.

"Right." The last thing Melanie wanted to do was answer a bunch of questions about where she'd been all summer. When they passed the arched doorway that led into the living room, Melanie peered in. A man with slicked-back hair wearing a dark suit was straightening the rows of folding chairs.

"Hi, Dad," Christina said. "Need help?"

"That's Uncle Mike?" Melanie exclaimed.

Grinning, he turned to face the girls. "Yup. Don't I clean up good?" he drawled. Crossing his arms, he rocked back on his heels and appraised the girls. "Wow. You're not the same tomboys I see running around the barns in jeans and dirty T-shirts, are you?"

Christina blew out an exasperated breath. "You and Uncle Will are so silly. Where's Mom?"

"Having a nervous breakdown somewhere. Thank goodness she got away to see Cindy yesterday. Otherwise I think she would have burst by now."

As they reached the kitchen Ashleigh dashed past, carrying a tray of shrimp into the dining room. Angela was arranging cups next to a punch bowl, while a woman in a black uniform with a white apron fixed a plate of fresh fruit.

"Yum." Melanie plucked several strawberries from the plate.

"You two make yourselves useful," Ashleigh said as she bustled back into the kitchen, wobbling slightly on her high heels. She wore a pale blue silk sheath and had brushed her brown hair into soft waves. She thrust a package of napkins at Melanie. "Fold these in half so they make a triangle, then arrange them like a fan on the dining room table."

Just as fast, Melanie passed them to Christina. "That sounds like something you'd be good at."

"Then you spread caviar on the crackers." Ashleigh pointed to a jar and a box. "Put them on the glass plate, and *don't* mess up your dress." She flashed the girls a grateful smile, then hustled back into the dining room.

"I'm eloping," Christina muttered as she opened the package.

"With who? Dylan?" Melanie teased. Grabbing the

box, she dumped some crackers onto the plate. Her stomach was growling and grumbling. And it wasn't just from hunger.

After today she'd have a new mom. *Stepmom,* she corrected. And if that weren't enough, on Tuesday she'd be starting eighth grade. Sure, it was the same school she'd gone to last year, but since she wasn't the same Melanie, it was going to be different.

Seeing Aynslee and Heather at the party would help. She'd need her old friends to make it through the first school day.

Opening the jar of caviar, Melanie wrinkled her nose. "Fish eggs. Only frogs should eat these."

"Then we'd better hurry and invite some," Christina said solemnly. Melanie giggled as she spooned a blob onto a cracker, and when Christina said, "You are so artistic, Mel. That reminds me of a hill of horse poop," Melanie burst out laughing.

Half an hour later all the people invited to the ceremony had arrived. The guest list was small, but Susan and Will had invited lots of people to the reception afterward. Melanie hoped there'd be someone famous for Aynslee and Heather to drool over.

Susan's best friend, Janice, was maid of honor, and Uncle Mike was Will's best man. Melanie, Ashleigh, and Christina sat in the front row. The rest of the guests were people from work and some old friends.

When it was time, the judge stood between two huge floral arrangements with Mike and Will on his left.

Then the wedding march began. Everyone turned to watch as Susan entered from the front hall.

Everyone but Melanie. *Maybe if I stare straight ahead, it won't happen,* she decided. *Susan will disappear, and I'll go home with Christina. I'll start school at Henry Clay and live happily ever after.*

Then she glimpsed her father out of the corner of her eye. As he watched Susan walk toward him he beamed like a little kid.

Melanie wanted to kick herself. *Stop being selfish,* she scolded. Why couldn't she think about someone else's happiness for once?

Tilting her head a teeny bit, she could see Susan. She was wearing an ivory-colored dress made of a soft material, and she looked beautiful. She radiated joy— just like Melanie's father.

As soon as the wedding was over, Melanie escaped to the downstairs powder room. Pulling a guest towel off the rack, she stuck it under cold water. Then she wrung it out and held it to her forehead.

What's wrong with me? she wondered. *Nerves? Or too many strawberries on an empty stomach?*

There was a knock on the door. "Melanie?" It was Susan. "Are you all right? You ran out of the room rather quickly."

"I'm fine. My stomach's a little upset."

The door opened a crack, and Susan peeked in. "Can I get you something?"

"No. You need to greet your guests."

"I have all night to do that. How about if I get you a roll and some soda?"

"Well, okay."

When Susan shut the door, Melanie checked her face in the mirror. Her blusher had been wiped off, and her lipstick was smeared. She looked like a ghost with a bad makeup job. Still, it was nice to know that so far her stepmom was okay.

"Mel, did you barf in there?" someone hollered from the hallway.

Melanie spun around as the door flew open.

"Hey, friend!" With a squeal of delight Aynslee pulled Melanie to her. Then, just as quickly, she pushed Melanie away and inspected her from head to toe. "Rad outfit. Kind of like you were attacked by a floral arrangement."

Melanie giggled. "Hi to you, too. Uh, it *is* Aynslee, right?" Her voice rose in a question as she got a good look at her friend. Aynslee's blue-gray eyes were ringed with dark eye makeup, and her lips were splashed with blood-red lipstick. She'd piled her hair on top of her head in a purposely messy knot, and she had on a black knit dress. The top was low-cut, the skirt thigh length and tight.

"Like it?" Throwing her arms wide, Aynslee circled as gracefully as possible in the bathroom. "It's the latest style."

"Gee, I must have missed it in Kentucky," Melanie murmured. She couldn't believe how mature her friend

86

looked—thirteen going on eighteen. "Does your dad know what you're wearing?" she asked. Even as liberal as Will was, she couldn't imagine him letting her set foot out of the house in such a skimpy outfit.

"Are you kidding? I had on this really dippy flowered dress over this one. Kind of like the one you're wearing. But there's no way I'm going to meet major rocksters dressed like Heidi. So as soon as we got here Heather and I ran up to your room, changed, and put on makeup."

"*Lots* of makeup," Melanie said.

Linking her arm through Melanie's, Aynslee pulled her into the hall. Since she was wearing black sandals with high, chunky heels, she towered over Melanie. "Let's go find Heather. She's probably checking out the food."

"I'm glad you're here, Ayns," Melanie said. "Now that we both have stepmoms, we can compare stories."

"Right. So, have any handsome dudes shown up yet?" Aynslee glanced from side to side as she propelled Melanie into the dining room.

"My dad and Uncle Mike."

Aynslee snorted. "Get real. Heather!"

Heather stood over by the table, filling her plate with an assortment of goodies. She was shorter and rounder than Aynslee, and her white dress bulged with curves that Melanie had never noticed before. Dismayed, Melanie glanced down at her own flat chest. How come her two friends had grown up over the summer while she'd stayed the same?

"Hi, Melanie." Heather gave her a big grin. She'd just eaten a strawberry, and red goop hung from her top lip.

Aynslee made a disgusted noise. "Honestly, Heather. No guy's going to be interested in someone with food all over her face."

"Then that will be all the more for you to flirt with," Heather said as she added three shrimp to her plate. "That's all she thinks about, Melanie. Guys."

"So where's the country mouse?" Aynslee asked, her gaze darting around the room.

"You mean Christina?" Melanie asked.

"Oh, I see her." She waved her hand at the corner where Christina was talking with Ashleigh. Frowning, Aynslee looked at Melanie, then back at Christina. "You know, dressed in those flowery things, you two could be twins. What happened to you on that farm, Mel?" Plucking the daisy from behind Melanie's ear, she twirled it in her fingers. "You don't look like yourself anymore. You don't *act* like yourself, either."

Reaching up, Melanie snatched the flower from Aynslee's grasp. "I guess that's because I've changed."

Heather had stopped eating and was staring at the two of them. "Melanie just got home, Ayns. Soon she'll be back to normal—and we'll all have fun again when we get to school. You know, glue Headmaster Howard's office door shut. Flush Grogan's memo pad down the john. Just like old times. Right, Mel?"

Wrong, Heather. All the old pranks sounded so petty,

Melanie couldn't believe she'd ever been part of them.

Just then Susan brought over a roll and soda. Melanie introduced her to Heather and Aynslee.

"So, Mrs. G., did your new husband invite any rock groups to your party?" Aynslee asked.

"As a matter of fact—"

Just then the front door burst open and a tall guy with dreadlocks marched in carrying an electric guitar. Aynslee's mouth dropped open, and Heather stopped in midchew. Even Melanie stared, totally speechless.

"It's King Cool!" Aynslee gasped.

"And his band," Susan said. "They're setting up on the patio. He's promised to play a couple of romantic songs for Will and me. After that you girls can request anything you want."

"I've got to meet him," Aynslee said. "Come on, Heather." Grabbing the other girl's hand, she dragged her into the hall.

Melanie turned to Susan. "King Cool! That is so great."

"Well, we wanted to do something for you and your friends. I knew he was one of your favorites."

"Thanks." Melanie's cheeks flushed, and she glanced away awkwardly. "And, Susan, I'm sorry if I haven't been very nice since I've been back."

She smiled gently. "I understand. It's going to be an adjustment for all of us. But I think we can do it."

Melanie returned her smile. "Me too."

10

ARM IN ARM, SUSAN AND WILL STOOD IN THE DOORWAY, waving as the last guests departed. Melanie sat below them on the top step, letting the night air cool the sweat off her face. It was almost midnight, and she was pooped.

Everyone had left except Christina, who'd decided to spend the night. She was upstairs getting ready for bed, which was where Melanie longed to be, too.

When the last car drove away, Susan and Will dropped their arms and groaned in unison.

"Thank goodness that's over," Susan said, slumping against Will's chest. "If I heard one more person say, 'You finally got him to tie the knot,' I was going to—"

"Puke?" Melanie cut in.

Her father looked down at her and frowned. "Melanie, such language." He stifled a grin.

"No, I was going to tell them that it was *you*"—Susan poked Will in the chest—"who begged *me* to get married."

Melanie shook her head. "He was desperate. Thank goodness he finally found someone who accepted his proposal."

Her father groaned. "So is this how it's going to be from now on? You two ganging up on me?"

"Yes," Melanie stated as she stood up and went inside. "So get used to it." Stopping in the hall, she glanced around. The house was a shambles. Plates and cups were piled everywhere. Crumbs, napkins, and sticky stuff dotted the rugs and floors.

"Let's leave it until tomorrow." Her father yawned.

"I agree." Susan had rings under her eyes, and her dress was wrinkled. Her dad had taken off his jacket and rolled up his sleeves. One shirttail was untucked, and his collar hung open.

"I think I'm going to elope," Melanie said, echoing Christina.

"I hope not anytime soon," Will said. "Ready for bed?"

"Yes." Standing on tiptoes, Melanie kissed him good night. "See you in the morning." Halfway up the stairs, she turned and looked down at Susan. "You too."

When she reached her bedroom, all the lights were off except the one in the adjoining bathroom. Christina was sprawled on the bed, dressed in one of Melanie's T-shirts, her eyes closed.

Melanie eased onto the edge of the mattress. "Chris?" she whispered.

Her cousin cracked one eye. "What?"

"I just wanted to tell you good night."

"Umph."

"And I'm going to miss you."

With a sleepy sigh, Christina rolled over onto her back. "I'm going to miss you, too. Everything all right with you and Aynslee? She kind of ignored you all night."

Melanie shrugged. "Sure. Aynslee can't resist rocksters. When she left she said, 'Cool party,' and promised to call."

"It *was* a cool party." Eyes drifting shut, Christina giggled. "Not like any wedding I've ever been to."

Melanie giggled. Then a lump caught in her throat. "I'm not worried about Aynslee. I mean, you're my best friend now, Chris, even if we won't be living together."

"You're mine, too."

"Promise me you'll call when you get back to Whitebrook?"

"Promise."

"And if I call you, promise you'll listen to my problems, no matter how stupid?"

"Promise." Christina's voice grew fainter.

"And of course I'll listen to your problems, too," Melanie said emphatically.

"Ummm."

"Not that you have any problems," she added.

93

When Christina didn't say anything, Melanie glanced down. Her cousin had curled into a ball. Her mouth hung slack, and she was breathing deeply.

Melanie inhaled shakily. Tomorrow would be here way too soon.

"Okay, Mr. Spunky, it's time for your introduction to the big city," Melanie told Trib the next morning. Lifting the saddle flap, she tightened his girth.

He squealed and crow-hopped in place. Being confined in the stall day and night was making him exceptionally frisky. The second she put her foot in the stirrup, he'd probably buck her off.

Not that a hard fall would make her feel any worse than she already did.

Christina, Ashleigh, and Mike had left at ten. Melanie had waved until the cab was out of sight, then said a cheery good-bye to Susan and her father. Not until she was halfway to the stable had she let the tears explode.

Seeing Trib had helped her feel better. She'd spoiled him with treats, hugged him until he pinned his ears, then brushed him until his coat shone. Still, her heart felt empty.

"You are riding this afternoon?" a polite voice inquired.

Melanie turned and saw Bettina Krueger. She wore a crisp sleeveless riding shirt and carried a helmet under her arm.

"Yes. Are you?"

"Yes. Would you like to ride together?"

Melanie grinned. "Sure. Trib and I can point out the sights. Only I have to warn you, Central Park is not exactly your typical trail ride."

"So I am told. I will meet you in five minutes."

As she put on Trib's bridle Melanie whistled the wedding march. Tonight she, Susan, and her dad would have their first family dinner.

A *family* dinner. She wondered how long her dad could stand being so domestic. She knew he loved jetting to California, wooing clients, and signing future rock stars. But just the idea that he was trying to be a better dad made her love him even more—and made her even more determined to try her hardest to make this family work.

Gustav clumped down the aisle, the sound from his huge hooves echoing through the building. Quickly Melanie buckled the throat latch and led Trib from his stall. He pranced down the aisle, then came to a screeching halt in front of the wooden ramp. Yesterday it had taken Melanie and Christina twenty minutes of coaxing and bribing to get him down it.

Melanie clucked. "Come on, Trib. You did this yesterday and it was no big deal, remember?" She tugged on the reins.

Bracing his legs, he stood firm.

"What's wrong?" Melanie asked impatiently. "You'd rather try the stairs? The fire escape?"

Bettina stood at the bottom of the ramp, looking up. "Perhaps he will follow Gustav."

Melanie blew a stray hair off her forehead. "Perhaps." The woman must think she was a total dunce around horses.

She turned Trib around and out of the way. Gustav clattered up the ramp. Bettina let him sniff noses with Trib. Immediately the pony's eyes sparkled with interest.

"Let's see if he will follow." Bettina swung Gustav around. Carefully the big horse picked his way down the ramp.

Trib almost pulled Melanie's arm off trying to keep up with him. "Whoa," she said firmly. When he reached the bottom of the ramp, he charged into the arena. Melanie scrambled after him, finally pulling him to stop in the middle of a circling group of riders.

"Only mounted riders are allowed in the ring," a woman declared.

"Uh, right." Melanie flushed bright red.

Trib had been so bratty in the ring yesterday—trotting fast with his nose stuck in the air—that she thought he'd crash into one of the steel poles. But at least only a few early-morning riders had been around to notice. Now the ring was crowded.

Melanie sighed as she led Trib toward the open doorway that led outside. Nothing like making a total fool of yourself in front of everybody.

"Now whoa." Melanie halted Trib beside Bettina,

who was already mounted on Gustav. The huge chestnut gelding stood quietly, a docile expression on his face.

Melanie gathered Trib's reins and stuck her toe in the stirrup. Swishing his tail, he took a step sideways. Awkwardly she hopped after him, hollering, "Whoa. Whoa."

Finally she yelled, "Whoa!" so angrily that half the riders turned to stare at her. Without a word Bettina angled Gustav next to Trib so that he couldn't go anywhere. Melanie pulled herself into the saddle, her face hot.

Hastily she found her stirrups, then guided him from the barn. When Trib saw the busy street, he stopped dead.

Bettina chuckled. "Your pony is quite *lebhaft*, as we say in Germany."

"He's wild, all right," Melanie grumbled.

Bettina laughed. "No, *lebhaft* means 'lively,'" she explained.

"He's that, too. He's used to living on a farm in Kentucky," she explained. "Every night during the summer he was turned out so he could eat grass, roll, and romp with his buddies. And during the day he used to go on trail rides in the woods and gallops over the pastures." Melanie sighed longingly.

"Ah." Bettina nodded. "And you miss it, too, I can tell."

"Yes." Melanie glanced up at her . . . way up. She

and Gustav looked as big as one of the statues in the park. "Your horse is so quiet. How come he doesn't mind all the noise and confusion?"

"He is used to being in a stall all day, then riding along roads or in an arena. In Germany land is precious. Horses are lucky if they get a few hours a day to play in a pasture."

"Then you'd better be the tour guide," Melanie suggested. "If Trib leads, we'll never get to the park."

"How far is it?"

"Just two blocks." Leaning down, Melanie patted Trib's neck. He was still staring at the taxicabs and buses, but he didn't seem as tense. "I think he's finally ready for his big adventure."

"Gustav will be happy to lead," Bettina said.

They started off. Melanie felt like a midget riding beside the tall Gustav and Bettina, but Trib didn't seem to notice. Arching his neck, he pranced and snorted like a mighty stallion instead of a small pony.

As they walked down the busy avenue Trib started at every pigeon and pedestrian. Suddenly he spied a hot-dog vendor standing by a white cart with a red-striped awning. Melanie spoke soothingly to him, and he was almost past when the wind caught the awning, snapping it like a sail. Tucking his tail, Trib leaped sideways onto the sidewalk, then clattered onto the metal doors of a closed loading chute.

The instant his metal shoes hit the metal door, he began to scramble. Melanie's heart flew into her throat.

It was just like what had happened to Milky Way, only then they'd accidentally stepped on a steel plate covering a construction hole. Milky Way had fallen hard, and before Melanie could react, a taxicab—

She cut off the image. She had to pull herself together and help Trib. Kicking her feet free of the stirrups, she did an emergency dismount. She put her hand on his neck to quiet him. "Stand," she said firmly, and this time he listened.

Under her fingertips, she could feel his muscles quivering. When he calmed down, she led him off the doors, one step at a time. Once they were back on the concrete, she breathed a sigh of relief.

"Quick thinking," Bettina praised.

Melanie was too shaken to reply. Only when they reached the park's sandy bridle path did she remount. "We'll circle the reservoir. It's really pretty," she told Bettina, her voice still shaky.

Trib broke into a jog, trying to keep up with Gustav's long stride. Melanie let him go, hoping that if he let out some energy, he'd settle down.

They trotted around the reservoir, peeling off onto another path that circled the ball fields. The fields were filled with players, the grassy areas dotted with picnickers. When they reached a quiet stretch of the trail, which was shaded by overhanging trees and bordered by shrubs, Bettina asked, "Is your pony ready for a canter?"

Melanie nodded. Though Trib's ears still rotated

wildly, he no longer viewed every biker and walker as a personal threat. "As long as we don't meet any killer squirrels or dive-bombing pigeons," she joked.

Squeezing her legs lightly against Trib's sides, she urged him into a canter. He was eager to go. Beside her, Gustav broke into such a smooth, collected canter that Bettina barely swayed in the saddle.

Melanie leaned forward into the two-point position as Trib's stride lengthened to keep up with the big gelding. The wind blowing against her cheeks smelled of newly mowed grass, and she pretended she was back in Kentucky, racing over the pastures with Christina.

She glanced at Bettina. She sat relaxed in the saddle, riding with a loose rein. Melanie was glad Bettina had gotten a chance to see her *riding* Trib instead of being dragged around by him. Otherwise, she was afraid, Bettina would never invite her to go with her again, and navigating Trib through the terrors of Central Park alone would not be fun.

They were nearing a thick stand of trees when Trib threw up his head and swerved toward Gustav. "Oh, no you don't," Melanie warned, driving him forward with her seat and legs.

Then, out of the corner of her eye, she saw two boys step from the trees. Their mouths were open as if they were laughing. When the horses started to pass, one of the boys raised his arm.

In a flicker of motion, Melanie saw something fly

through the air. It sailed over her head, landing on Gustav's flat, solid rump.

Instantly Melanie knew what it was. "Firecracker!" she screamed, but her cry was lost in the loud crack of the explosion.

11

THE SHARP BANG WAS DEAFENING. STARTLED, GUSTAV leaped in the air like a circus horse. Bettina lost her balance and flew off backward. Reins dangling, Gustav bolted down the path. Trib took off after him.

Everything happened so quickly that for an instant Melanie froze. Then, using a pulley rein, she hauled Trib in a tight circle and headed him back toward Bettina.

She was sitting up, gingerly inspecting her left ankle.

"Are you all right?"

"I think so."

Melanie glanced toward the side of the path. The two boys were looking surprised, but when they saw Melanie glaring at them, their expressions turned cocky.

"You jerks!" Melanie said. "You could have hurt someone!"

"How were we supposed to know the horse would freak?" one of the guys asked, and Melanie realized that she knew them both: Robert Walgreen and Pete Smith.

They were her age and went to Manhattan Prep. Many nights in the past she'd escaped from the townhouse and she and Aynslee had met them. With a shudder she thought about some of the stupid stunts they'd pulled in the park—painting graffiti on sidewalks, kicking over trash containers, spraying people with soda.

She turned Trib toward them. "Well, you should care, because I'm telling your parents."

"Oooh." Robert shivered in mock fear. Then, when he realized who it was, his face broke into a grin. "Melanie? When did you join the safety patrol?"

"Not Madwoman Mel!" Pete said, chuckling.

Angry, Melanie turned Trib around. There was no use talking to them. They didn't care what they'd done.

Bettina hadn't moved. "Please find Gustav," she said. "Make sure he's all right."

"I will." Mel trotted Trib down the bridle path. Fortunately Gustav hadn't gone far. He was munching grass by the side of the trail. Trib whinnied excitedly when he saw him.

Gustav lifted his head. A piece of rein about ten inches long dangled from the right side of the bit. When he bolted, he must have stepped on the reins and broken them.

Melanie slid off Trib and grabbed up the long end of the reins. Then she walked around Gustav, checking to make sure he was all right. Leading both horses, she walked back to Bettina. She was standing, but all her weight was on her right leg.

"Is Gustav all right?" Bettina asked.

"Fine. How about you?"

"I think my ankle is sprained. If you can help me on . . ." Her voice trailed off when she saw the snapped reins. "Well, this is a dilemma."

"Bettina, I'm so sorry." Melanie felt the blood rush to her face.

She raised her brows. "It is not your fault. My seat was not secure, and my reins were too loose for control."

"No, I don't mean that. I mean, I *know* those boys."

"So? Did you ask them to throw the firecracker? Stop apologizing so we can start heading back to the stable. Once I put ice on my ankle, it should be fine."

"Okay. I'll help you up onto Gustav and lead you back."

"Do you think you can make it?"

"Sure." Melanie smiled convincingly, though she knew her boots would rub her heels raw. Then she had an idea. "In Kentucky I used a horse named Pirate to pony racehorses to and from the track."

"Pony racehorses?"

She explained what it meant. "Should we try it?"

Bettina grinned. "Why not? I've always wanted to be a jockey."

Holding on to Gustav's neck, she hopped to her

horse's left side. Melanie laced her fingers together and put them under Bettina's bent left knee.

"One, two, three, jump." She hoisted the older girl as high as she could, then Bettina pulled herself the rest of the way.

Melanie patted Gustav's neck. He hadn't budged. "You are a good boy."

Bettina laughed. "Unless a firecracker explodes on his butt."

Holding the long piece of Gustav's rein, Melanie mounted Trib. When they started back the way they had come, the pony pricked his ears eagerly. "He's been here only three days and already he knows he's headed home," Melanie said.

"That's because horses can smell where they've been," Bettina explained. Gustav walked happily beside Trib, adjusting his stride to the pony's as if he knew he had to go slower.

"I still can't believe those jerks," Melanie said. "I'm definitely going to call their parents." Had she really once acted as stupidly as those two boys?

It took them twice as long to return to the stable. Melanie untacked and brushed both Trib and Gustav, and after making sure they were cool, she went into the office to check on Bettina.

Her leg was propped on a chair with an ice pack draped over the ankle. She'd taken off her helmet, and her long blond braid hung over her shoulder.

"How is it?" Melanie asked.

Bettina lifted the ice pack. The ankle was swollen, the skin black and blue.

"Are you sure it's not broken?"

"Yes. Jonathan checked it."

"Gustav's in his stall. I told him you'd be riding again soon."

She nodded, but her face was pale, her eyes drawn. "Thank you for taking good care of him."

Jonathan bustled in with a man dressed in riding clothes. "Your cab's outside, Ms. Krueger." Jonathan shot Melanie an annoyed look, as if it were her fault one of the boarders had fallen. "We'll help you out to it."

Melanie stepped out of the way. Bettina struggled upright, then draped her arms around the men's shoulders. In the doorway she stopped and looked back at Melanie. "Thank you for the ride," she said. "*Auf Wiedersehen.*"

Melanie waved good-bye. With a sigh, she left the office to put her tack away. Melanie knew Bettina didn't think the accident was her fault. Still, she, Melanie, was obviously bad luck. In fact, the way things were going, she wouldn't be surprised if *auf Wiedersehen* meant "I hope I never see you again."

The phone rang five times during dinner, and five times her father jumped up and went into the office to answer it. Melanie and Susan could hear him talking all the way in the kitchen.

"How was Trib?" Susan asked, trying to keep the dinner conversation going, but Melanie could tell she was listening to her with only half an ear. After all, since she was involved with the company, she was interested in what her husband was discussing, too.

"Fine. We had a long ride in the park."

"Sorry." Her father bustled back into the kitchen, giving them apologetic looks. "From now on the answering machine can get it. Okay?"

"Sure, Dad." Melanie speared a soggy strawberry. Since Angela had the day off, they were eating wedding party leftovers.

"Melanie was just about to tell me about her ride."

"Did you go with friends?" her father asked.

Melanie nodded. "Yes. A new boarder at the stable. Hey, did you sign that rock group you were talking about last night?" she asked, changing the subject so that he wouldn't question her about the riding. She didn't want to tell her dad about Bettina's accident at the park.

As soon as she'd gotten home Melanie had called Robert's and Pete's parents, whom she knew. Both had been skeptical when she'd told them the details, but they'd said they'd speak to the boys. Melanie figured that meant they wouldn't do anything, but she felt better having called. Maybe if someone had been more concerned about her reckless behavior, Milky Way never would have been killed.

"I'm meeting their manager tomorrow," Will said, launching into the details.

Relieved, Melanie reached for the shrimp. She didn't have Bettina's phone number, so she couldn't call to see how she was. She'd have to get the number from Jaylaan tomorrow.

"So how about it, Mel?"

Her father's question brought her back to the conversation.

"How about what?"

"Tomorrow, after school, do you want to go with me and Susan to meet Nick and the Knights?" he asked excitedly.

"Uh, thanks, but I'd rather ride."

"Oh." Her father's enthusiastic expression died.

Melanie bit her lip. She should have said yes. But at the same time, if she didn't ride, Trib would be cooped up in his stall all day and night.

"Maybe we can see them sometime this weekend," she suggested. "When I have more time."

"That's a good idea," Susan agreed. She smiled fondly at Will. "Hey, Dad, remember that your daughter has her own interests."

"I know. But what she sees in that furry, four-footed creature, I'll never know," he said, his tone playful.

Twenty minutes later, when they had finished eating, Susan said, "I rented a video for tonight. *The Dream Machine*. What do you think?" She glanced excitedly at Melanie and her father.

"Uh, isn't that for little kids?" Melanie asked.

"Well, it's PG-thirteen, and you're twelve."

Melanie and her dad started to laugh.

Susan's smile faded. "Uh-oh. It sounds like I made my first big stepmom mistake."

Leaning across the table, Will squeezed her hand. "That's okay. You didn't know Melanie's been watching grown-up films for years."

They cleared the table. Melanie rinsed the dishes while Susan put away the food. Her dad went back to the office to listen to his messages.

"You know, Melanie, since I'm new at this, I'm going to make some major mistakes," Susan said.

"That's okay. I'm new at it, too. And, hey, you're doing fine."

"Mel! There's a message from Aynslee. She wants you to call her back."

Melanie dried her hands on a dishtowel. "She probably wants to see if we have any classes together," she told Susan. "I'll call from my room," she hollered to her dad as she ran down the hall.

She raced up the steps and into her room. Out of breath, she threw herself on her bed and dialed Aynslee. Her friend answered after the first ring.

"What's up?" Melanie asked as she slumped back onto her pile of pillows.

"Lots. I hear you ratted on Pete and Robert."

Melanie's heart skipped a beat. "Yeah, I called their parents," she said cautiously.

"I thought they were your friends."

"Look, Aynslee, Robert and Pete did something stupid and dangerous."

"That's not the point," Aynslee said, her voice low. "The point is how you treat your friends. And ratting on them is not my idea of friendship."

"Maybe they aren't my friends anymore," Melanie said.

This time Aynslee was quiet. Melanie wondered what was going through her mind. Was she trying to decide whose side she was on?

"Robert called a few minutes ago and asked me to give you a message, Mel. Do you want to hear it?"

"No. That's—"

"He said, 'Thanks for getting us in trouble. We won't forget what you did.' Do you get their drift?"

When Melanie didn't say anything, she repeated, "Do you get their drift, Mel?"

"Yeah, I get it."

"It means you're on their hate list."

"Big deal, Ayns." She hung up with a bang. So much for sharing class schedules.

Crossing her arms over her chest, Melanie lay quietly on the bed. Her gaze drifted to the framed drawings of Pirate.

Even though it seemed like an eternity, she'd left Whitebrook only three days ago. Did Pirate finally realize she was gone? Did he miss her?

She hoped Kevin had ridden him over the holiday.

Kevin . . . She wondered what he was doing right now. Should she call him and tell him what had happened? He'd understand why she'd had to call Robert's and Pete's parents. Besides, it would be nice to hear his voice.

Propping herself on one elbow, she reached for the phone. But her hand stopped in midair.

She was wrong. Kevin *wouldn't* understand about Pete and Robert, because he'd never understand why the two jerks had been Melanie's friends in the first place.

With a groan Melanie rolled onto her stomach and buried her face in her pillow. There was no one she could turn to. She couldn't tell Susan and her dad her problems, because they wanted everything to be perfect. She couldn't confide in Christina and Kevin, because they were too far removed from New York and the Roberts of the world. And she couldn't talk to Aynslee, because her friend was mad at her.

"You might as well face it," she mumbled to herself. "From now on, you're on your own."

12

THE NEXT MORNING, WHEN THE CAB PULLED UP IN FRONT OF the Lincoln School, Melanie's breakfast did a quick slide to her feet.

"We're here, miss," the driver said politely. Melanie handed him the fare, then scooted from the cab. A few girls were walking down the sidewalk, talking excitedly. Several cars were parked in front, dropping students off.

Melanie didn't recognize anyone. Not that she expected to. Last year she'd hung out with Heather and Aynslee or kept pretty much to herself. She hadn't been on any teams or joined any clubs. In fact, she'd cut classes as often as she could get away with it, and after school she'd headed to the stable.

This year she was going to work harder at keeping up her grades. Still, afternoons wouldn't be much different. She'd promised Trib she'd groom and ride him every day.

Smoothing the navy skirt and white blouse of her uniform, Melanie hurried up the steps, her backpack over one shoulder. The school had been built in the early 1900s. It had heavy doors, marble floors, mahogany wainscoting, and high ceilings with ornate woodwork.

Her homeroom was B49. Melanie made her way upstairs. Since the school was private and fairly small, there was a good chance Aynslee would be in her home-room.

She was. Melanie spotted her immediately. She was sprawled in her chair, talking animatedly to Heather while chewing gum. Her hair was still piled on her head in a messy nest, but since she wasn't wearing makeup, she looked more like the old Aynslee. Melanie eyed her cautiously. She had no idea if Aynslee was even going to talk to her.

Heather saw her first. She waved gaily. "We saved a seat for you," she called. "Though once old man Leonard shows up, he'll probably give us assigned seats."

As Melanie walked across the room Aynslee studied her with a bored expression. Then she puffed out her cheeks and blew a big bubble.

Melanie slid into the wooden chair, waiting for her to make some snide remark. But she only popped her bubble and said, "Glad to have you back, Melsie."

"Thanks, Ayns. Do you think we'll have many classes together?"

As the three girls compared schedules Melanie felt her tension slowly drain away. Then Mr. Leonard came in and started explaining all the new rules. He passed out contracts. "These clearly spell out the school regulations. They should be signed by you and your parents and returned tomorrow."

Melanie tucked the contract into her pack. When homeroom was over, she headed to English class. After that was Algebra I, then right before lunch she had art with Ms. Wokowski. She was looking forward to it.

The morning went quickly. Neither Heather nor Aynslee was in her first two classes, but when she entered the art room Aynslee waved hello.

Somehow, since homeroom, she'd managed to paint her fingernails purple with pink stripes. Melanie sat on the stool next to her and plunked her backpack on the big table. "Early art project?"

Holding up her hand, Aynslee fanned out her fingers. "Beauteous, huh?"

"When did you have time to do them?"

"PE. I told Mrs. Fennerman I have a *sprained ankle.*"

Melanie stiffened, suspecting a trap. But when Aynslee asked, "Hey, how is your friend with the sprained ankle?" her tone was so sincere, Melanie thought she might really be interested. Maybe Aynslee had decided to be on her side after all.

"I don't know. I'm going to call her from the stable this afternoon."

"Nice nails, Aynslee," someone commented, and

then Ms. Wokowski came in and Melanie turned her attention to the art teacher.

For fifty minutes they worked on basic shapes and shading using pencils, then markers. When class was over, Melanie was gathering her things when Ms. Wokowski came up to her. "I'd like to invite you to the first meeting of the art club, Melanie. It's tomorrow, right after school."

"Art club?" Melanie repeated, flustered yet flattered. The club members were serious artists, and joining was by invitation only. "Yes. Sure. I'll be there."

"Good."

When Ms. Wokowski left, a grin slowly spread over Melanie's face. She glanced around for Aynslee, but she'd already left. Then she noticed the folded note stuck under her backpack.

Meet me in front of the office, it said. *I have a surprise for you.*

Melanie recognized Aynslee's handwriting. Puzzled, she refolded the note and put it in the front pocket of her pack. What did she mean by a surprise?

Knowing Aynslee, it could be anything. Maybe she'd ordered pizzas to be delivered for lunch.

Melanie hurried down the steps to the front hall. It was empty, since most of the girls were headed to the cafeteria located at the back of the school. At the bottom of the steps she turned in a circle, hunting for Aynslee. As she turned toward the office she paused in front of the oil painting of Abraham Lincoln that hung on the wall by the door.

She blinked, not sure if she was seeing things. Had someone drawn a mustache over Lincoln's mouth? Stepping closer, she stood on tiptoes to get a better look.

Yes. Whoever it was had used black marker. Then Melanie noticed the square of white paper tucked behind the picture. Glancing over her shoulder to make sure no one was looking, she pulled it out.

Another note.

It was only one word: *Gotcha*. Underneath were Robert's and Pete's signatures.

A gasp made Melanie whirl around. Mr. Howard, the headmaster, stood right behind her. "What in the world?" he sputtered as he stared in horror at the painting. Then he cut his eyes to her face, and his expression was murderous.

Melanie's mouth opened, but nothing came out.

"In my office, Miss Graham," he ordered.

"But I didn't have anything to do with it!" Melanie protested.

"In my office!" he thundered.

She followed him past the counter, past Miss Horowitz's desk, past the computer terminal, and into his small office.

She might as well face it. There was no use trying to convince the headmaster that she was innocent. For one thing, she had a history of pulling pranks, and of course she had always lied when confronted. But the other reason was that she really *wasn't* innocent.

He left the door open. Turning, he held out one hand. "Give me your backpack, please."

Without a word Melanie pulled it off her shoulder. He rifled through it, triumphantly holding up a black marker. "I thought so. Still, I'm amazed that even you had the nerve to pull a stunt like that on the first day of school."

"I'm amazed, too, sir," she said.

He bristled, but when he saw her expression wasn't brash, he frowned in puzzlement. "Can you explain to me *why* you wrote on the painting?"

"No, sir." She dropped her gaze. No matter what she said, it wouldn't make sense to him. Because even though she hadn't drawn the mustache, she was still to blame.

If she hadn't tattled on Robert and Pete, the picture wouldn't have been defaced. It was like a big line of dominoes—once the first one was knocked over, the rest went with it.

She'd been the first domino.

Around and around the small arena they went—figure eights, serpentines, half halts, extended trot—until Trib finally stopped and wouldn't budge.

Exhausted, Melanie leaned both hands on the pommel. Trib's sides heaved and his nostrils flared. Sweat dotted her forehead, and the muscles in her legs quivered.

Still, Melanie didn't want to stop. The first day of school had been the pits. Howard had called her father and left a message. That meant going home wouldn't be any better.

She longed to ride to the park. But she knew getting Trib through the congested streets would be almost impossible. Bettina was going to be off her feet until the weekend, which meant she had to find another riding partner or stay in the arena.

Heaving a sigh, Melanie nudged Trib into a walk. "Come on. You need to cool down before I bathe you."

Trying to make a game of it, she steered him around the steel support poles as if they were in a pole-bending race. Still, she could tell Trib was bored. Two other riders worked their horses in the arena, so at least he had company. But the riders were older women on elegant Thoroughbreds, intent on mastering some difficult dressage movement, so they weren't interested in a grumpy girl on a pudgy pony.

"Maybe tomorrow we can hook up with a group that's going to the park," she told Trib. "Oh, wait. I've been invited to an art club meeting. I'll have to ride afterward."

Then it would be too late to ride to the park, and they'd have to spend another boring afternoon in the arena.

"Maybe I should skip school," she muttered. "Then we could spend the whole day at the park." After today she wasn't sure she even wanted to go back to school.

She knew that Aynslee had been the one to draw the mustache and plant the note. But the strange thing was, Melanie wasn't angry at her. Deep down she knew that Pete and Robert had to get revenge. Maybe it was better this way. Now they were even.

She hoped.

Half an hour later Trib was back in his stall and Melanie was trudging the last block to the townhouse. Her lower back throbbed, and her thighs felt like Jell-O. But facing her father would be ten times worse than any physical pain.

She spotted his car parked on the other side of the street. *Great.* He was home already, probably expecting another cozy evening with his family. Instead he would find a message from the headmaster.

As she tromped up the steps she pulled the house key from the pocket of her breeches. Unlocking the door, she opened it slowly, slipped inside, shut it behind her, then tiptoed upstairs. She could hear voices coming from the kitchen. She didn't stop long enough to hear what they were saying.

Quickly she dropped her backpack on the bed and ran into the bathroom, shedding her clothes on the way. She turned the shower on full force. By now they must know she was home, but when her dad came upstairs she'd pretend she couldn't hear him.

After locking the bathroom door, she stepped into

the tub. As the water pelted her face she thought about what she should say. Obviously she couldn't tell the truth. That would mean explaining too many unexplainable things.

It wasn't as if her father wasn't used to calls from school. It was just that she hadn't been home even a week. He'd be so disappointed no matter what explanation she came up with.

"Mel?" Someone knocked on the bathroom door.

"Dad?"

"It's me."

"I didn't think you'd be home so early. I'll be out in a minute."

"Good. I need to talk to you."

Melanie finished her shower. As she dried off she listened for sounds outside the door. Knowing her father, he'd gotten tired of waiting and had gone downstairs. Right now he was probably sitting in the kitchen asking Susan what he should do.

She combed her damp hair, whisking her fingers through it until it stood up in all directions. Then she wrapped the towel around her body and opened the door.

He was sitting on her bed, staring at the photo of the two of them that she kept on her bedside table. He was still dressed in his work clothes—a stylish linen sport coat worn over a light blue shirt.

"I thought you'd gone downstairs."

"You mean you *wish* I'd gone downstairs." Slowly

he set the picture on the table. "So, are you going to explain your side of it before I go in and see Mr. Howard tomorrow morning?"

Melanie clutched the towel tighter around her. "Gee, he wants you there already?"

"Well, after spending so much time with him last year, we're old friends."

"Right." Melanie nodded to her bathrobe, draped over the back of her desk chair. "May I?" Grabbing it off the chair, she went into the bathroom and put it on.

Her heart felt heavy. Her dad acted like someone had beaten him over the head. He'd always been confused and upset when she'd gotten in trouble, but this time he seemed even more lost. Maybe if he yelled and screamed like regular fathers, it would be easier to take.

She took a deep breath, then opened the door and sat beside him. "It's not as bad as it sounds," she said, trying to keep her voice light. "It was a practical joke. You know, to liven up that dreary old school a little."

Her father gazed at her, his head tilted and his brow furrowed as if he was trying hard to understand.

"I mean, you've seen that painting of Lincoln. He looks like he's about to die. We only used washable marker. The mustache wiped right off."

"We?"

Oops. Melanie bit her lip. "I mean me," she clarified. "It's Aynslee, isn't it?"

"Look, Dad, even if it was, I'm not going to tattle."

He let out his breath slowly. "Mel, I thought you'd changed."

"I have."

"Then prove it to me. No more pranks. No more calls from school, or I'm not going to let you see Aynslee anymore."

"Okay." Melanie tried to sound upset.

"And if that doesn't work, if you still get in trouble, I'm going to have to send Trib back."

Melanie gasped. "What?"

Her father nodded firmly. "No more riding. Every afternoon you'll have to come right home."

Melanie stared at him openmouthed. "You wouldn't."

"I would." He stood up, his face red, his expression pained, as if his decision was as hard on him as it was on her. "I haven't been firm enough with you in the past, Melanie. Well, that's going to change. Dinner's in ten minutes. We expect you to be prompt."

Even after he'd gone, Melanie's mouth still hung open. This time she knew her father was serious.

13

IT WAS FRIDAY MORNING. MELANIE SAT ON THE STOOL IN art class, hunched over her paper as she sketched the arrangement in the middle of the table. It was a still life created by eighth graders. Instead of a bowl of fruit and a pitcher, the girls had arranged a Nike shoe, a tube of lipstick, and a carving knife in front of a stuffed squirrel from biology class.

As Melanie concentrated on her drawing she thought about the week. For two whole days she hadn't gotten in any trouble. When Will and Susan had gone out to dinner with clients the night before, she'd even stayed home and studied.

The only problem had been fitting in visits to Trib. Wednesday and Thursday afternoons she had stayed after school until five-thirty with the art club, working on the pottery wheel. Melanie had become so engrossed in molding the spinning clay, she'd almost forgotten about the pony. When the club broke up, it was too late to go to Clarebrook. Today she'd make it up to him. She'd called the stable and arranged to be included in a group riding to the park at four.

Melanie's thoughts were interrupted by the sound of someone cracking gum in her ear. She twisted around. Aynslee was standing behind her, watching her draw.

"Pretty good, Mels, except that squirrel looks dead."

"It is dead." Melanie continued drawing. She hadn't spoken to Aynslee since Tuesday—not because she was mad, but because she had nothing to say to her.

"So, you want to do something this weekend?" Aynslee asked.

Melanie's pencil point stopped in the middle of the squirrel's whisker. "Like what?"

"Heather's spending the night Saturday. We could make it a mini slumber party and rent a video or something."

"It's the 'or something' I'm worried about." Melanie finished sketching the whisker, then feathered the squirrel's tail so it looked bushy.

"Look, ever since my dad found me climbing out the window at midnight, he's been watching me like a hawk. The 'or something' would probably be as tame as reading the juicy parts from a romance novel."

"Let me think about it."

"Suit yourself." Aynslee sauntered off. Melanie

watched her from the corner of her eye. Was this Aynslee's way of making up?

When the bell rang, Melanie went to lunch. When she reached the cafeteria she headed for a table in the far corner. Since Tuesday she'd been eating with several of the girls from the art club. Because this was her first year in the club, she didn't really know them, but it was better than eating alone.

"Can I sit here?" Heather asked as she plunked her tray next to Melanie and slid in beside her. Her bangs flopped in her eyes, reminding Melanie of a sheepdog.

"I think you already are."

Heather burst into giggles. "You're right. I am." She reached for Melanie's zippered lunch bag. "Hey, whatcha got?" she asked, looking inside. "You're still not eating party hors d'oeuvres, are you?" she asked, pronouncing it "orders."

"No, tuna on whole wheat."

"Yum." Heather smacked her lips. "Do you want to trade? I've got Salisbury steak."

"No, thanks."

Aynslee sat on the bench across from Melanie. She had an apple and a glass of orange juice. "Begging food again, Heather?"

"I was offering to trade."

"Yeah. Your idea of a trade is a roll for an entire lunch. You're going to turn into a fat pig if you don't watch out."

Melanie peered over her carton of milk. Aynslee had

a nasty tone to her voice, but Heather didn't seem to notice.

For a second Melanie wondered how she and Aynslee had even become friends. Then she remembered. She had been just as smart-mouthed as Aynslee. She and Aynslee had had one other thing in common— mothers who had left too early and fathers who had worked too hard.

"So what did you decide about Saturday?" Aynslee gave Melanie a long look.

"Probably. Still, I'm not sure." She leaned over her lunch bag. "First I have to know if we're even."

Aynslee nodded. "Yeah. I was impressed. I expected you to tell Howard it was me who drew the mustache on Lincoln." She smiled. "You passed the test. Maybe the new Mel isn't so bad after all."

"Or maybe you're turning into a new, improved Aynslee," Melanie joked.

"Me?" She pointed to her chest, an indignant expression on her face. "What's there to improve?"

Melanie laughed, glad that she and Aynslee were back on teasing terms. She hated to admit it, but she was lonely, and right now Heather and Aynslee were her only friends in New York.

"Boy, am I glad to see you!" Melanie greeted Trib that afternoon. Pulling a carrot from her back pocket, she swung open the stall door.

Trib instantly pinned his ears, not at all happy to see her. Swinging away from the door, he stuck his head in a corner and switched his tail.

"Hey, is that any way to say hi?" Melanie asked. She held out the carrot. He rolled one eye at her but didn't move.

Melanie frowned. He'd always been cantankerous when she came in with the bridle. But this afternoon something was different.

Then she noticed his stall. An oval had been tramped in the straw as if he'd been walking in circles all night. And on one side of the wall there were long scrapes in the wood. When she peered closer, they looked like teeth marks.

"Trib? What's going on?"

She moved closer, and he cocked one hind hoof threateningly. Immediately Melanie jumped back. She'd never seen him act like this.

"Are you mad I didn't come yesterday?" He switched his tail again. "That must be it. Well, I'm sorry." Lifting up the carrot, she took a bite. "I guess you're so mad you don't want any of this, right?"

Taking another bite, she made exaggerated chewing noises. "Mmm. This must be the best carrot in all of New York."

He flicked an ear toward her. Again Melanie held out the carrot. This time he turned around, sniffed it, and took it from her palm. By then Melanie had the lead rope over his neck, so he couldn't move away. As he munched the carrot she put the halter on. Then she stepped back to check him out.

Something *had* changed. She ran her fingers down his legs. They were thick and swollen. His ankles had stocked up from standing in the stall so long. His coat was matted from lying in manure.

But it was more than that. Trib had always been full of tricks. Bratty, yes, but never mean. Now there was a sour look in his eyes instead of his usual devilish gleam.

And it was all her fault.

"Oh, Trib, I promise I won't skip an afternoon again. You don't deserve to be locked in this stall all day like some kind of prisoner." Picking a currycomb from the grooming bucket, she swiped at the crusted manure on his side and belly. He fidgeted and twitched, but finally she saw his lips wiggle with pleasure.

Melanie grinned. "Feel better? And just wait. We're going with a group to the park. It should be lots of fun."

She finished brushing him, then picked out his hooves. Twenty minutes later he was tacked up and ready to go. Fortunately, another horse was heading down the ramp the same time as Trib, and he followed it willingly.

Once he was downstairs, Melanie was glad to see him perk up. A group of horses and riders had gathered by the open garage door. While she waited, Melanie trotted a few circles in the arena to settle Trib down. She didn't want him running off in front of everybody. But he was so quiet, she finally let him stand with the others.

Jaylaan came out of the office, a clipboard in her hand. She called off names, checking them when people said "here." Then Jonathan came down the upstairs ramp leading Gustav.

"Is everyone ready?" he asked Jaylaan as he led the big mare into the arena.

"Yup." She hadn't called Melanie's name.

Hesitantly she raised her hand. "Uh, you forgot me."

"I did?" Jaylaan asked with exaggerated surprise. "Oh, right. Melanie Graham. How could I forget *you?*"

Melanie's face colored.

"Let's go," Jonathan said. "Single file until we reach the park, then ride in twos, staying behind me at all times."

Melanie held Trib back until the last horse and rider had left. She didn't want anyone watching if Trib pulled some dumb stunt.

He walked quietly all the way to the park. Not exactly *quietly*, Melanie corrected herself. *Cautiously*, as if he was afraid the cars were going to attack. Once they reached the park and his hooves touched the dirt path, Melanie let out a sigh of relief. The problem was that she was too tense. Every time she heard the scrape of a metal shoe on pavement, it reminded her of the accident.

The horses paired off. Melanie found herself next to a skinny lady with a pug nose who was riding Bailey, one of the school horses. She was holding the reins so tightly, Bailey's mouth hung open.

"My first trail ride," the woman confessed.

Gee, I never could have guessed. "Just relax and have fun," Melanie told her. "And, uh, you don't need to hold your reins so tight. Bailey's really quiet."

The woman let the reins slacken a hair. Her arms and body were so stiff, she looked like an ironing board.

"When my pony feels like he's going too fast, I hold my reins in one hand." Melanie showed her. "Then I grab a hunk of mane with the other."

"Good idea." Loosening her death grip, the woman held on to the mane. Bailey snorted with relief.

After they had ridden in the park for about an hour, the group headed back to the stable. The sun was setting, and rush hour traffic had slowed.

Melanie let Trib wander around outside the stable to cool off. Every once in a while he pulled her toward a green sprig that had pushed its way through the concrete. With a heavy sigh, Melanie leaned against the brick wall. The trail ride hadn't been very exciting, but at least Trib had gotten out. She knew she had to say something to Jonathan about lessons. She couldn't spend the rest of the year riding with beginners.

"Come on, Trib, it's getting dark." Reluctantly Melanie led him inside. She wanted to find Jonathan and talk to him before she chickened out.

She put Trib away, promising to come early in the morning. Then she went to look for Jonathan.

She poked her head into the office. "Has anyone seen Jonathan?"

Jaylaan didn't even look at her. "He's downstairs."

"Thanks." Melanie wondered if Jaylaan would ever change her feelings toward her.

As Melanie went down the ramp the slick soles of her boots slid on the worn wood. Flattening her hands against the wall, she inched the rest of the way down, pausing at the bottom to get her bearings.

She hadn't been in the dungeon since Milky Way's death. It was actually the cellar of the old livery stable and hadn't been designed for horses. The ceilings were low, the stalls narrow, and even though small windows had been cut out of the stone walls, it was dark, especially at night, when only a few dim bulbs lighted the aisles.

Melanie shuddered. She'd forgotten how creepy it was.

"Jonathan?" she called.

"Back here."

Melanie walked slowly down the aisle, greeting the lesson horses, who were contentedly munching hay from racks. She found Jonathan checking one of the horses' legs. When he glanced up and saw who it was, he frowned. "What do you want?"

Melanie took a deep breath. "I'd like to start taking lessons again."

"I'm booked solid."

Melanie didn't know what to say. Was he telling the truth?

"Can you put me on the waiting list?"

He straightened. "Maybe there'll be room for you next spring."

His blunt answer made Melanie flush. For once she

133

was glad the dungeon was so dark. Jonathan wouldn't see how upset she was.

"Why don't you just say it? After what happened, you don't want to teach me."

He clenched his jaw. "Maybe you're right. Maybe I'm having a tough time being nice after what happened to Milky Way."

Tears sprang into Melanie's eyes. "I know I was stupid and irresponsible," she said, trying to keep from crying. "But you don't know how many times I've wished I could take back that night."

"Oh, really? Then how come you never even apologized?"

Melanie was taken aback. "I didn't, did I," she whispered.

"Nope. Daddy whisked you away, bailing you out one more time." He sounded disgusted.

"No wonder you've been so angry."

Turning, he patted the horse on the neck, then bent to check its other leg.

"I'm sorry, Jonathan," Melanie blurted. "You have no idea how sorry."

Melanie was so upset, she was trembling. Spinning, she raced down the aisle. She turned the wrong corner, running into a sticky mess of cobwebs. She batted them away, whirled, and found the ramp. Halfway up she slipped and fell hard, bruising her knees.

"Melanie!" Jonathan jogged down the aisle. "Are you all right?"

For a second she knelt on the ramp until she'd choked back her tears. Then she pulled herself to her feet. "Fine."

"Listen . . . there might be an opening in a couple of weeks."

She glanced at him in surprise. "You mean it?"

"Yup. People can change, right?" He gave her a half smile.

"Right." Melanie blew out a relieved breath. "Thanks," she told him as he turned to go back to the stall.

She checked Trib one more time, put away his halter, and even said good-bye to Red, the night watchman.

When she left the stables, it was dark. All the way home she thought about the good things about New York—being with her dad, riding Trib, the art club, and taking lessons again.

Still, she couldn't help but feel homesick for Whitebrook. She'd loved everything about living at the farm, and she missed her friends and Pirate.

She hadn't talked to her cousin since Monday. It would be fun to find out how Christina's first week at school had been.

Unlocking the townhouse door, Melanie dropped her things on the hall floor and ran upstairs to the phone.

"Mel!" Christina's voice was so bubbly, it brought tears to Melanie's eyes. Thank goodness someone was happy to talk to her.

"I'm so glad you called," Christina rushed on. "I've got so much to tell you. Katie and Chad split up, Dylan asked me to go to the eighth-grade dance, Sterling jumped three-six during the lesson yesterday, Faith won a big stakes race—"

"That is so great!" Melanie cut in, excited to hear all the news. But as her cousin rattled on and on, a sinking feeling grew in her stomach. She might really miss Christina. But even though she hated to admit it, Christina didn't miss her. And why should she? She had tons of friends, a horse she loved, and a wonderful place to live. In fact, Melanie couldn't think of one thing that Christina didn't have.

When Christina paused, Melanie quickly asked, "How's Pirate?" before her cousin caught her second wind.

"Good. At the beginning of the week he was feeling kind of down, so Ian decided to give him a new job."

"A new job?"

"Yeah." Christina giggled. "Baby-sitter."

"What?"

"Ian turned out a real bratty colt with Pirate. This colt was biting and kicking the other yearlings. Ian thought maybe Pirate could teach him a little respect."

Melanie couldn't believe it. "But Pirate's blind. Didn't the colt hurt him?"

"Are you kidding? It took about ten minutes for Pirate to show the little demon who was boss. Now, thanks to Pirate, the colt—we call him Rambo—has perfect manners."

"What about Pirate?"

"It was good for him, too. They play together like brothers."

"Oh." Melanie was glad Pirate was happy, but it would have been nice to know that someone missed her.

"How's Trib?" Christina asked.

"Oh, great!" Melanie said with forced cheerfulness. "Everything's great." She told her about art club and riding in Central Park, then realized that was all she had to say.

"Too bad you aren't here," Christina said. "Mona's planning a weekend ride sometime in September."

"Gee, I'd love to hear about it, but Dad and Susan just came home. Call me Monday and tell me how the dance went."

"I will. And you call me anytime and tell me about, well, anything," Christina said.

"I will." Hanging up, Melanie fell back on her bed. Susan and her father weren't home, but she hadn't wanted to listen to Christina anymore. She especially didn't want to hear the details of a weekend ride she wouldn't be going on. Clearly she had to try harder to make friends here in the city. Reaching for the phone, she dialed.

"Hi, Ayns," she greeted. "It's Mel. My dad says I can spend the night Saturday. I'll be there at seven. And, hey— I'm feeling kind of down. So let's have fun. Okay?"

14

EARLY SATURDAY MORNING SUSAN AND WILL CAME DOWN to breakfast wearing shorts and running shoes.

"You two are up already?" Melanie asked as she dumped cereal in a bowl.

"Yup." Her dad grinned. "We're going running in the park." He wore a sweatband around his forehead. Susan had her hair pulled back in a ponytail.

"Right." Melanie eyed her father skeptically.

"We are." Will puffed out his chest, touched his toes, then did a deep knee bend. When he straightened, he grimaced dramatically.

Susan laughed. "Take it easy, tiger," she said, then told Melanie, "I've been trying to get your father to run with me for months."

"I've been too embarrassed to go with her," Will confided. "Now that she's married to me, I figure she can't dump me when she sees how out of shape I'm in."

"Oh, you're not that out of shape," Susan teased as she poked his stomach.

"Are you going to Clarebrook?" her father asked.

"Gee, how'd you guess?" She was dressed in breeches and boots.

He winked. "Didn't I ever tell you that my grandfather was Sherlock Holmes? Anyway, we thought we'd jog that way and stop by to see Trib."

Melanie swallowed too fast, and milk went down the wrong pipe. When she started to choke, her father patted her on the back.

"The signs they put in restaurants say you're really not supposed to thump people on the back when they choke," Susan said.

Raising one hand, Melanie waved them both away. "I'm okay," she gasped. She wiped her mouth, and when she caught her breath she said, "Don't stop by. I'm going for a long ride this morning with a group. We're leaving right away. Maybe I'll see you at the park."

"Okay." Her father cheerfully accepted her lie.

Ducking her head, Melanie quickly finished her cereal. She didn't want Susan and Will anywhere near the barn. Her father wouldn't understand Jaylaan's cool attitude. Plus Bettina was coming around to see Gustav, and she might let something slip about the accident in the park.

Melanie's stomach tightened when she realized

how smoothly she'd started lying again. And the lies were mounting up. Sure, she told them for a reason—she wanted her father to think everything was perfect. But lies were like dominoes, too. Something was bound to go wrong sooner or later.

"I've got to run upstairs and get a sweater," Susan said. "Meet you outside."

"Aynslee called last night," Melanie said when Susan left. "She wants me to spend the night."

She waited for her dad to say no, so she could recite the list of reasons she should go.

"Are you sure that's a good idea?" he asked. "Remember our talk about getting in trouble."

Melanie felt an angry flush creep up her neck. "Aynslee's my friend, so you're going to have to trust me, Dad."

"All right." He held up a palm. "It's just that Susan and I have been invited to a dinner party on Long Island, and we were hoping you would come with us. The hosts have a boy your age—and if that doesn't interest you, they also have a heated pool."

Melanie wrinkled her nose. She knew how that went. The boy her age would resent being stuck with her, pool or no pool. The guests at the party would be a bunch of business executives and wanna-be stars. "I think I'd rather go to Aynslee's. She's planned a cool evening."

"Okay. I'll give Aynslee's dad a call—to tell him where we'll be that night, just in case," he added quickly. Bending, he kissed her on the forehead. "Maybe we'll see you in the park. I'll be the one collapsed on the bench, wheezing."

As soon as he left, Melanie felt her insides unwind. She knew she should tell him the truth—she hated his parties, and going to Aynslee's wouldn't be much better. But he wanted to believe she was happy. And if she forgot about Whitebrook and tried harder to love New York, maybe she would be.

In case the two stopped at Clarebrook, she took her time getting to the stables: slowing to watch a police officer pull over a van without a license plate, buying a hot pretzel from a vendor, picking handfuls of grass that grew in the cracks of the sidewalk.

It was almost ten when she reached the stable. Trib was standing in the corner of the stall, his head down.

"Look what I brought you." She held out a handful of grass, and his head popped up. When she put it in his feed tub, she noticed the tub had grain in it. And below it on the ground was an untouched flake of hay.

Trib hadn't eaten his breakfast.

Alarm bells went off in Melanie's head. Trib was a world champion chow hound. What was going on?

Ignoring his get-lost expression, she went over and ran her fingers along his side. She could feel his ribs.

Had he eaten at all lately?

She held out more grass. He ate it unenthusiastically, then stuck his head back in the corner.

Yesterday he hadn't acted right. This morning he

142

seemed worse. She needed to find out what was going on.

She thumped downstairs in her boots and went into the office. A line of riders waited in front of the desk. Melanie scooted past them.

"Jaylaan, who's been feeding Trib all week?"

Head bent, Jaylaan continued writing on the paper. "Wait your turn, please."

"This is important. Trib's sick. Just tell me—"

"Go to the back of the line, please."

Melanie snatched the pen right out of the older girl's fingers. Leaning close, she whispered, "I want to know who's been feeding Trib."

That got her attention. "Bobby. He's outside."

"Thank you." Melanie smiled as she handed back the pen, then ran out the front door. Bobby was a hulking guy about twenty who must have been hired over the summer. He was sweeping the sidewalk in front of the stable.

"Bobby? Are you the person in charge of feeding the horses upstairs?"

He nodded.

"Has the pinto pony been eating all his hay and grain?"

"Pinto?"

"You know, black-and-white patches."

"Oh, *that* one." Stopping, he leaned on the end of his broom. "The one that always tries to bite me."

"That's him. Well?"

"No, the last couple of days I've had to throw out his morning feed."

Melanie sucked in her breath. "Why didn't you tell me?"

"I told Mr. Franco. He said not to worry about it, that since the pony was new, it would take him a while to get used to the different feed."

You still should have told me! Melanie clenched her teeth, trying not to scream. She wanted to reach up and wring his thick neck even though she knew it wasn't his fault. It was that stupid new manager's fault.

"Thanks." Spinning, she hurried back to the stable. Maybe Mr. Franco was right. Sometimes horses were really picky about new feed, but Trib usually ate anything.

She hurried upstairs, forming a plan. She'd ride Trib to the park with his halter on under his bridle. Then she'd find a beautiful patch of grass and let him graze. If that didn't tempt him, she'd know something was wrong for sure.

When she climbed the ramp, Bettina was hobbling down the aisle.

"Hi!" Melanie's face broke into a huge grin. She'd never been so glad to see someone. "How's the ankle?"

"Still too sore to ride, but I had to come and check on Gustav to make sure he is getting good care."

"I know what you mean." She told him about Trib while they walked to the pony's stall. Bettina tsked when she saw him.

"Perhaps, like the manager said, it is the strange feed, and some sweet grass will whet his appetite. But if your plan does not work, you call me and I will give you the number of my veterinarian."

"Thanks. I will."

Picking up her grooming bucket, Melanie went into the stall. After talking to Bettina, she felt a little better. She brushed Trib with care, combing out his mane and tail until they were soft and fluffy.

She tacked him up, putting the bridle over the halter. Then she snapped the lead line onto the halter and tied it around his neck. Just in case he broke his bridle, and for her own sense of security.

Now, if only she could get him to the park . . .

Trib was so balky, it took twenty minutes to go one block. Finally Melanie gave up, dismounted, and led him the rest of the way. He followed more readily. Still, anytime a horn honked or a siren wailed, he jumped, stepping on her heels and toes.

By the time they reached the park, Melanie could hardly walk. She stopped in the first grassy area that wasn't taken by Frisbee throwers or smooching teenagers. Dropping down under the tree, Melanie took off her boots. Her little toe was bruised, her heel rubbed raw.

"I am *not* walking you back," she told him. "You are a horse, and I am riding you."

Ignoring her, he chewed the grass greedily. Melanie sighed with relief. At least she knew he wasn't sick.

Taking off her helmet, she let her head fall back against the trunk, then closed her eyes. The sun through the leaves dappled her face with light. The earth felt cool under her toes. The grass smelled sweet. No wonder Trib was happy to be outside.

Opening her eyes, she watched him munch. Too bad it was so difficult to get to the park every day. Still, she'd have to try, even if it meant quitting the art club.

"Time to head back, Tribbles," Melanie finally told him after about half an hour. It had to be past noon, and her stomach was growling. She put on his bridle, tightened his girth, then let down her stirrups.

As soon as she was on his back she could feel him tense. Warily he glanced around, suddenly finding every bird and jogger suspicious.

Melanie thought she knew what was going on; she'd read some of Christina's books on horse behavior. Since horses were herd animals, they felt more secure in a group. When she was on the ground, Trib considered her a herdmate who would help keep an eye out for danger. But the moment she mounted he thought he was alone, facing the dangers of the wild by himself.

She patted his neck. "I'm still here, Trib. And I'll try my best to protect you. Deal?"

They made it back to the stable in one piece, though Trib was still so jumpy, she trotted him around the arena for fifteen minutes, trying to calm him down. It only made him worse. When she halted him, he pawed the dirt flooring and yanked his head down against the pressure of the bit, dragging the reins through her hands.

"Easy, bud." Melanie spoke softly as she dismounted. Running up her stirrups, she walked him around the arena a little while longer.

When it was time to put Trib back in the stall, he put on the brakes. Melanie rolled her eyes. "You are the most obnoxious animal," she declared, meaning every word. She was tired, hungry, and sick of his antics. She struggled with him for fifteen minutes. Finally he calmed down enough for her to groom him.

"Tomorrow we'll go to the park again and just hang out. I'll pack a lunch, so we can stay longer. Okay?"

Trib blew softly into her palm. She hugged him around the neck, then said good-bye, hoping she could keep her promise.

"Gin," Melanie said laying her hand on the Harlands' living room floor. Groaning, Aynslee rolled onto her back. Heather stared at the cards as if puzzled. "But I thought they all had to be the same color."

Aynslee groaned again. Melanie burst out laughing. Spending the night at Aynslee's had been a good idea. They'd done totally stupid stuff—played with the Ouija board, painted their toenails, baked brownies and eaten them all.

"Okay, you guys, ready to do something exciting?" Aynslee said. "That's what you wanted, right, Mel?"

"That depends. What did you have in mind?" Melanie asked, her trouble-detecting radar switching on.

Aynslee lowered her voice. "How about going up on the roof?"

"The roof?" Heather repeated. "But you don't have a roof. You live on the sixth floor of an apartment building." Aynslee lived in a luxury apartment building with carpeted hallways and vases of fake flowers set on tables and illuminated by wall sconces.

"I'm talking about the roof of the whole building. Ten stories up. We'll be able to see forever!"

"You can do that?" Melanie asked.

"Sure. There's a door that leads right to it."

Heather and Melanie exchanged dubious glances.

Aynslee jumped to her feet. "Come on. There's a full moon tonight. It'll be awesome."

"Are you sure it's allowed?" Melanie repeated, getting to her feet.

"Of course. Why are you so worried?"

"Because my dad's being really strict all of a sudden. He says if I get in trouble one more time, I'll be grounded forever."

"So when did you turn into a wimp?" Aynslee asked as she headed for the front door, Heather right behind her. Since she was wearing only a nightshirt, Melanie grabbed her jacket before following them out.

"Should we tell your parents?" Heather was asking.

"I told them already. When I got the sodas." Aynslee led them out of the apartment. Ignoring the elevator, she gestured for Heather and Melanie to follow her down the luxurious hallway to the back stairs.

Melanie hung back. Had Aynslee really told her parents? Well, going up to the roof sounded like fun. And she hadn't been having much fun lately.

"Let's go for it," Melanie said. Giggling wildly, the three girls ran up the stairs in their bare feet. At the top of the last landing they collapsed in a heap, still laughing hysterically.

Finally Aynslee pulled herself up. Putting a finger to her lips, she led them into the hallway of the tenth floor, then to a heavy metal door marked Emergency Exit.

"That's it?" Heather whispered.

"Yup." Aynslee pushed it open. The stairs were narrow and dark and led straight up to an angled door latched from the inside.

Aynslee went first, Melanie behind her. As they slowly climbed the steps Melanie felt the pulse beating in her wrists. Behind her she heard Heather's ragged breathing.

Reaching up, Aynslee slipped the latch. Then, putting both palms on the door, she pushed it up.

A rush of cool air poured over Melanie's face. Eagerly the three climbed out. The roof was wide and perfectly flat, and since a high brick wall surrounded it, Melanie could see that it was perfectly safe.

When she looked up into the sky, she broke into a smile. Aynslee had been right. It was a full moon, so huge that Melanie felt as if she could reach up and touch it.

Throwing her arms wide, she titled back her head

and twirled in a circle. "Let's do a moon dance!"

"A moon dance!" Heather and Aynslee repeated as they spun with her, faster and faster, until Melanie's head grew dizzy from the swirling stars.

A loud clunk from the stairwell made Melanie jerk to a stop. "What's that?" she asked, swaying drunkenly.

Aynslee and Heather had stopped, too, and were staring at the open door.

"Who's up there?" a gruff voice hollered. "No one's supposed to be up there at this hour!"

"It's Magruder!" Aynslee hissed.

"The super?" Heather squeaked.

Melanie grew rigid. "Are we going to get in trouble?" Running over to Aynslee, she grabbed her wrist. "Aynslee, you said it was okay to come up here."

Aynslee shrugged. "I've done it a million times."

Dropping Aynslee's wrist, Melanie glanced around. She couldn't get in trouble. Her father would send Trib back to Whitebrook for sure.

She had to get off the roof before someone caught her!

15

MELANIE SPRINTED TO THE EDGE OF THE ROOF, LOOKING FOR a fire escape.

"Melanie!" Aynslee grabbed her arm and swung her around to face her. "Get a grip. He won't catch us. Magruder's too wimpy. Now be quiet and listen."

Melanie held her breath, but her heart was pounding so furiously, she couldn't hear anything else.

She forced herself to look at the door. The light from the hall below streamed up to the roof. Still, Magruder didn't pop his head through the opening.

"See? He's scurried back to his office to call the building manager." Without letting go of Melanie's arm, Aynslee strode to the door. "Come on. We'll be back in the apartment before he figures out who it was."

The three charged down the narrow stairway, across the hall, and into the emergency stairwell. As they pounded down the steps Melanie's legs felt like rubber.

They reached Aynslee's apartment just in time to see the elevator going past, headed to the tenth floor.

"See?" As Aynslee opened her apartment door, she began to laugh. "Didn't I tell you it would be okay?" she asked.

"No!" Pushing past her friend, Melanie stormed into the apartment. "What you told us was that it was okay to go up there."

"Well, you said over the phone you wanted to have fun."

"I told you I couldn't get in trouble." Ducking, Melanie picked up her shoes off the floor, then whirled to face Aynslee. "You lied to me."

Aynslee frowned. "You told me you'd get grounded. Big deal. You were grounded a hundred times last spring. It didn't bother you then—you just sneaked out when your dad left."

"Only this time it's different. My father told me if I got in trouble, he'd send Trib back."

"Send Trib back? You didn't tell me that."

Furious, Melanie stepped around Aynslee and marched into the hall. "Thanks for a great time, guys," she said. "But do me a favor—never invite me again."

"Mel, you can't leave," Heather said. "You're only wearing jammies."

Melanie pointed her shoes in Aynslee's face. "Don't mention any of this to your parents," she warned. "As far as you know, we had fun all night, then I went home in the morning. Right?"

Aynslee and Heather nodded in unison.

Shoulders squared, Melanie gathered her stuff, then jogged silently to the stairway. She didn't dare take the elevator, in case she bumped into someone.

"Bye, Melanie!" Heather called as if nothing had happened.

Melanie opened the door. Before it closed behind her, she heard Aynslee yell, "I didn't know about Trib. I'm sorry, Mel. Really sorry."

But it was too late for apologies.

The lobby was empty. Outside the building, a police car was pulled up along the curb. Zipping her jacket, Melanie raced for home. It was only two blocks, and she had traveled the distance many times in the dark.

As she ran, her anger slowly evaporated in the cool night air. She'd never been that mad, that panicky before. Last spring she would have been frightened in a delicious kind of way if the super had caught them on the roof.

Now it was different. She couldn't lose Trib. Without him she'd be lost.

When she got to the townhouse she fumbled for the key in her jacket pocket. She opened the door, then locked it behind her. Leaving the lights exactly as they were, she hurried upstairs, shutting her bedroom door.

Susan and Will would be back from their party late. They'd never know she was here. Melanie slipped off her shoes. Exhausted, she fell onto the bed. Pulling the bedspread around her like a cocoon, she promptly fell asleep.

She awoke with a start. Sunlight streamed through the window, so Melanie knew it was morning. She held her breath and listened. The townhouse was silent.

Good. If she hurried, her plan would work.

Jumping out of bed, she quickly smoothed back the spread, then tiptoed into the bathroom. She checked her face in the mirror. It was smudged with dirt, and dark circles ringed her eyes. Was it the face of a liar?

Turning on the shower full blast, she climbed in. A minute later she heard a knock, then Susan called, "Good morning!" loudly enough that Melanie knew she'd opened the door. "We didn't hear you come in."

"I didn't want to wake you up," Melanie hollered. "Be out in a minute."

"Did you have breakfast?"

"Not much."

"Good. I'll fix omelets."

Whew. So far so good. Melanie shampooed her hair, then stood in the shower, arms hanging, letting the hot water pound her chilled body.

When she knew she couldn't stall any longer, she turned the shower off and got out. Fifteen minutes later, wrapped in her bathrobe, she went down to the kitchen.

Susan was cooking omelets in a skillet. Her father

154

sat at the table, sipping orange juice and reading the newspaper. "Hey, slumber party girl, want some fresh-squeezed juice?" He nodded to a small pitcher.

"*You* made fresh-squeezed juice?"

"I did. We got a super-duper juicer for a wedding present, and I'm determined to use it."

Melanie choked back a giggle. Her dad was so goofy, it was going to be even harder to lie. No, it was going to be easier. More than anything, she wanted him to stay happy.

"So how was the sleepover?" Susan asked. She wore a silk kimono, and even in the morning, without makeup, she looked pretty and fresh.

"Fun. Though we stayed up *really* late."

"How come you came charging in and jumped in the shower?" her dad asked. "Did the Harlands run out of hot water?"

"Uh, no." Melanie looked convincingly sheepish. "We sort of experimented with hair color last night. When I got a look at it in my bathroom mirror, I just about died. I didn't think you'd like it."

Will leaned back in his seat, a pleased smile on his face. "You mean you're through being my blue-haired girl?"

"Right. Blue hair's out, tattoos are in," Melanie joked.

Susan brought over an omelet and slid it onto Melanie's plate. "Mmm. Looks delicious." She poured herself some juice and took a sip. "And this is heavenly.

Maybe you guys should get out of the music business and start your own restaurant."

"Speaking of business . . ." Will told her a little bit about who had been at the party the night before.

Melanie exhaled with relief. They'd bought the story. She was home free.

"The Michados have a home on the coast of California," Susan said. "They want us to fly out for a long weekend. Combine business and pleasure."

"That sounds fun." Melanie ate the last bite of omelet. "Angela can stay here with me."

"He invited all three of us." Susan sat down on the chair opposite Melanie, an excited expression on her face. "We want you to come. We can go to Disneyland, the San Diego Zoo—"

"But I can't go," Melanie interrupted. "I've got school, and I can't leave Trib."

"Sure you can leave Trib," her father chimed in. "Hey, we were all going to work hard on being a family, remember?"

"I know, but there's no way Trib can stay cooped up in his stall for four days."

"Get Aynslee to ride him. Or one of the new friends you've met at the stable."

With growing horror Melanie stared at her father. What he suggested was reasonable, except for two big problems—she and Aynslee weren't friends anymore, and her only friend at the barn had a sprained ankle.

And the worst thing was that she couldn't tell him.

"Well, yeah, I guess I could do that," she fibbed. "Let me ask around. This coming weekend?"

"Right. We'll leave early Friday morning and get back late Monday night. I'll call the school and set it up." Her father was grinning. "You wait. We're going to have so much fun, you won't even miss Trib."

"I bet you're right!" Melanie said, standing so abruptly she knocked the pitcher over. Orange juice spilled over the newspaper, across the table, and onto the floor.

"I'm so sorry!" Melanie pressed her hand to her mouth.

"Hey, just an accident," her father said, eyeing her with a puzzled expression.

Susan was already mopping the table with paper towels. "I'll clean it up."

"Thanks. I've got to get to Clarebrook." Melanie fled from the kitchen. When she reached the top of the stairs, she hung onto the banister and gulped deep breaths. She had to get hold of herself. She had to figure out what to do.

As she dressed in her riding clothes she realized she needed to go with them on the trip. Hadn't she decided to try harder? Maybe they'd have a great time, and when she came home she'd start fresh.

But first she had to make sure that Trib was all right. Then she'd have to find someone to ride him for four days. Maybe Jonathan could fit it into his busy schedule.

She ran all the way to Clarebrook. Since there were no lessons Sunday morning, the stable was quiet. Bobby was raking the arena, smoothing out the soft dirt in preparation for later. There was no one in the office.

"Bobby, did he eat last night?" Melanie called.

"Who?" He looked at her in total confusion.

"My pony. The black-and-white one."

"Right." The light dawned. "The one that kicks. No, he didn't eat."

Oh, no. When Melanie got to Trib's stall, she immediately knew he was worse. He stood in the same corner, his head hanging. His eyes were dull, and when she patted him, he didn't react at all. She checked his feed tub. It was full of grain. He hadn't eaten a thing. *Time to call the vet.* She hurried to the office and dialed Bettina's number, crossing her fingers that she would be home. She was, and she gave Melanie the number, also offering to come right over.

Melanie called Dr. Benhi, the veterinarian. The answering service said they would page her.

She paced the floor. Finally, after what seemed like hours, a woman answered. Melanie told her what was wrong. She said she'd be there in fifteen minutes.

By then Jaylaan had sauntered into the office.

"When Dr. Benhi comes, please show her where Trib's stall is," Melanie said.

"Who's Dr. Benhi?"

"The vet."

Jaylaan propped one hand on her hip. "We use Dr.

158

Kennedy," she stated. "I'll have to tell Jonathan."

Melanie propped her own hand on her hip. "Tell Jonathan. I don't care," she said right back.

Bettina arrived first. "Poor Trib. He is no longer *lebhaft*."

"You can say that again." Tears pricked Melanie's eyes as she stared into the pony's stall. Flies had settled on his rump, and he didn't even switch his tail. "And it's my fault."

"Your fault?" Bettina raised her brows. "How is that?"

"He's my responsibility, and I failed him."

"You knew something was wrong. You just didn't know what. That's the doctor's job." Bettina's tone was so gentle and understanding, it made Melanie feel worse.

"Now, don't get so gloomy that you can't help Dr. Benhi," Bettina said. "She will ask many questions. You see, she treats the horse's mind and soul as well as his body."

"She does?"

"Yes."

"That's good, because I think Trib's soul is really sad."

"Bettina! Good to see you again."

Melanie turned. A middle-aged woman in jeans, work boots, and a polo shirt strode down the aisle carrying a medical bag. She was smiling broadly, and she radiated such confidence that Melanie felt slightly better.

"You're Melanie?" she asked as she set her bag in front of the door.

"Yes. And this is Trib."

Dr. Benhi peered in the stall. Reaching in her bag, she pulled out a stethoscope. "Hold him for me, please, and while I'm checking him over, I want you to tell me everything."

And Melanie did—starting with the day they'd left Whitebrook.

"Interesting," Dr. Benhi said.

"What? What did you find?" Melanie exclaimed.

"I meant your story is interesting."

Stepping into the aisle, the vet pulled out a syringe and several tubes from her bag. "I need to take blood samples."

Melanie grimaced and held tighter to the lead line. "Trib hates needles."

"The way he's feeling, I don't think he'll even notice." Expertly she took two vials of blood. "There. I'm done."

Melanie ruffled Trib's mane, then unhooked the lead line. "What do you think is wrong with him?"

"I won't know for sure until the blood work comes back. It'll take a day."

"But what do you think?" Melanie persisted.

"I think your pony is severely depressed. All his vital signs are normal. No indication of fever, pain, or colic. Of course, his blood work could show an infection or illness that I can't detect."

"Depressed?" Melanie repeated. "You mean, horses can get sad like humans?"

"*Sad* isn't the word. Their bodies shut down. From what you tell me about Trib, he's a very smart, very aware pony with strong opinions. The change in environment was too much for him. He went into mental and physical overload."

"Then it *is* my fault."

"Of course not." She patted Melanie's shoulder. "With time he'll adjust. We have to make sure he doesn't get dehydrated; we have to try different feeds, and you need to continue exercising him as much as you can."

"How much time?"

"It could take a month or more before he really settles in. Let's try putting something in his ears to muffle the sounds. From what you say, he's hypersensitive to noise."

"A month or more!" Melanie couldn't believe it.

"Think how long it would take a person from the country to adjust to life in the big city. And people understand about cars and sirens. Ponies don't."

"Poor Trib." After the vet and Bettina had gone, Melanie sat down in the cramped stall. She tried to imagine how Trib must feel. "Oh, Trib, how could I have done this to you? I never should have let you come here. The city is no place for a pony raised on a farm."

Suddenly it dawned on Melanie what she had to do. She stood up and buried her face in his mane.

If she wanted Trib to get better, she had to send him home.

The blood work came back normal. Melanie was right: Trib needed to go home. With a heavy heart, she told her father and Susan at dinner Monday evening.

Setting his fork on the edge of the plate, Will said, "Now, let me get this straight. Trib—a pony—is so depressed he needs to go back to Whitebrook?"

"What's so odd about an animal's being homesick, Will?" Susan asked. "Animals have a whole range of emotions. In fact, there are animal psychologists, and vets are putting dogs and cats on medication for depression."

Melanie's father held up his hands. "I'm not arguing. I'm just trying to understand."

"Yes. He needs to go home. I'll call Christina tonight," Melanie said.

"I'll call them," Will volunteered. "That way I can make sure they understand that they should pick him up before we leave for California."

Reaching over, Susan put her hand on Melanie's. "I'm sorry, Mel. I know how much you love Trib."

"Yes, but if the pony's not suited to New York, then we'll find one that is." Her father chucked her under the chin. "What do you think? Is there a horse at Clarebrook you like?"

Melanie forced a smile. "That's all right, Dad. I think

I'll forget riding for a while. I was invited to join the art club, and since it meets after school, it's too hard to do both."

"Art club? Great! Why didn't you tell us?"

"I just did." Smiling politely, Melanie asked to be excused. "If it's all right, I'd like to do my homework at the stable. Dr. Benhi says the best thing for Trib is company."

"Okay. I'll come pick you up at nine."

She nodded. Slipping out of the chair, she left the kitchen and went upstairs. As she gathered her things in her backpack she spotted Kevin's Blue Jays cap hanging on her bedpost. She put it on. Maybe it would help her get through the next couple of days.

When she reached the stable, Red unlocked the door to let her in. Earlier she'd gotten permission from Jonathan to be at the stable after hours.

"Hey, Trib. Look what I brought you." She held up a bag of carrots. He ate them with more excitement than she'd seen in two days. Maybe the cotton in his ears was helping. Still, he was a far cry from the feisty pony she used to know.

Setting her pack against the wall, she fluffed the straw and sat down. As she pulled out her algebra book she told Trib about going home. "I bet Joe will come right away," she said. "By Wednesday you'll be chasing Sterling around the pasture. Christina will bring you treats, Kevin will call you an ornery thing, Ashleigh will . . ."

Two tears plopped on her book cover. "Oh, Trib, I wish I were going with you. But I can't, because then my father would be as sad as I am." She jumped up and draped her arm around the pony's neck. He was so warm, so solid.

And she was going to miss him *so* much.

"Melanie?"

Startled, Melanie jerked her head up. Her father stood in the doorway of the stall. "Dad? What are you doing here so early?"

Her father came into the stall, a confused expression on his face. "This is Trib? The same pony you rode at Whitebrook?"

Melanie nodded.

"I didn't recognize him. He was so lively when I saw him, so full of spirit, so . . ." His voice trailed off, and he shook his head. "Oh, Mel, I can't believe I was so dense. I can't believe it took a depressed pony to make me realize what was wrong with *you*."

"Me?" Melanie tensed. What was her father talking about? She'd worked so hard to act as though everything were all right. "I'm fine, Dad. I mean, I'm going to miss Trib, but I'll adjust. Really."

"When I visited you at Whitebrook you were so happy. Everything excited you. This past week, since you've been home, I've watched that happiness die, that excitement fade."

"No, that's not true," Melanie protested. "I've enjoyed being home with you, and Susan's great."

164

He held up his hand to stop her. "Melanie, quit telling me what you think I want to hear. Ever since you've been home you've been like a robot, smiling and saying, 'Everything's great, Dad!' when I know it can't be. I almost like the old blue-haired Melanie better. At least when you yelled and argued, I knew how you were really feeling."

"But everything's been okay," Melanie said, starting to cry.

"Oh, Melanie." He put his arms around her and let her sob against his chest. "I'm sorry it took me so long to see how unhappy you are. I'm sorry it took me so long to realize that I can't have everything *I* want. Take the California trip. I wasn't thinking about what was best for you. I just thought about what I wanted."

He gave her a squeeze, then held her at arm's length so he could see her face. Melanie hastily wiped her eyes.

"I didn't call Ashleigh and Mike yet," he told her. "Let's go do that now. When I reach them, I'm going to ask if they'd still like to have you stay with them for the school year."

"What?" Melanie gasped.

"I realize now what you tried to tell me days ago— you don't belong in New York, Melanie."

"What about all that family stuff?"

He grinned. "I'll always love you more than anything—no matter where you live."

"Oh, Dad." Fresh tears poured down Melanie's cheeks. "I love you so much. And I'm so sorry it didn't work out. I wanted it to work out. I tried hard, but—"

"But your heart belongs at Whitebrook?"

She nodded. "Yes. For the first time I made really good friends—kids I could talk to and joke with. And the horse stuff was awesome. Every morning I'd wake up and know I could take a lesson, or pony a racehorse, or go on a trail ride."

Her father chuckled. "I get the picture."

"That doesn't mean I haven't enjoyed being with you and Susan!" she repeated quickly.

"I know. But it's pretty obvious our jet-setting lifestyle isn't what you want."

This time Melanie laughed. "Maybe someday."

Her father started for the door to the stall. "Ready to go?"

"Let me get my books together and say good-bye to Trib. I'll meet you downstairs."

When he left, Melanie picked up Kevin's hat. Smiling, she put it on her head, then turned it backward.

She went over to Trib and gave him a big hug. "Guess what? In a couple of days you'll be rolling in your pasture, and I'll be riding Pirate. We're going *home*, Trib. We're really going home."

ALICE LEONHARDT has been horse-crazy since she was five years old. Her first pony was a pinto named Ted. When she got older, she joined Pony Club and rode in shows and rallies. Now she just rides her Quarter Horse, April, for fun. The author of over thirty books for children, she still finds time to take care of two horses, two cats, two dogs, and two children, as well as teach at a community college.